ROBERT SWINDELLS

The Shade of Hettie Daynes

CORGI

THE SHADE OF HETTIE DAYNES
A CORGI BOOK 978 0 552 55708 5

Published in Great Britain by Corgi Books,
an imprint of Random House Children's Books
A Random House Group Company

This edition published 2008

1 3 5 7 9 10 8 6 4 2

The Random House Group Limited supports The Forest Stewardship
Council (FSC), the leading international forest certification organisation.
All our titles that are printed on Greenpeace approved FSC certified
paper carry the FSC logo. Our paper procurement policy can be found at
www.rbooks.co.uk/environment

Mixed Sources
Product group from well-managed
forests and other controlled sources
www.fsc.org Cert no. TT-COC-2139
© 1996 Forest Stewardship Council

Set in12/16pt Century Old Style
by Falcon Oast Graphic Art Ltd.

Corgi Books are published by
Random House Children's Books,
61–63 Uxbridge Road, London W5 5SA

www.**kids**at**randomhouse**.co.uk
www.rbooks.co.uk

Addresses for companies within The Random House Group Limited can
be found at: www.randomhouse.co.uk/offices.htm

THE RANDOM HOUSE GROUP Limited Reg. No. 954009

A CIP catalogue record for this book is available from the British Library.

Printed in the UK by CPI Bookmarque, Croydon, CR0 4TD

Bethan touched Alison's sleeve, pointed. 'There, *look*.'

Alison's eyes followed the trembling finger. She started to shake her head, then gasped. 'Yeah, there *is* something . . . a shape . . . *does* look like . . . crikey!'

Bethan eased the camera out of her pocket.

Alison plucked at her jacket, whispered, 'What you doing? Don't leave me.'

''S OK.' Bethan touched her friend's hair. 'Need to get a shot, see – proof.'

Alison stared at the motionless wraith, so like the black trunks behind it. *It's a tree*, she told herself. *Just a tree, except* . . . That pale smudge, just where you'd expect a face to be. And another one, smaller, farther down. A *hand*?

The flash made her jump. A brief whirr, and Bethan was back beside her, brandishing the camera. '*Got* her!' she hissed. 'Right in the middle of the frame . . .'

Also available by Robert Swindells,
and published by Random House
Children's Books

Abomination
Blitzed
In the Nick of Time
Nightmare Stairs
Room 13 *and* inside the Worm (omnibus edition)
Timesnatch

For Frank Hingston
". . . that things are not so ill with you and
me as they might have been, is half owing to the
number who lived faithfully a hidden life . . ."
George Eliot

ONE

Harry squeezed his sister's arm. 'Are you *sure* you want to see her?'

Bethan snorted. ''Course. Wouldn't be here if I didn't, would I?'

The boy shrugged. 'Want you to be sure, that's all. She's seriously spooky, and you *are* only ten.'

'So? You're two years older, big deal.'

'OK, come on.'

The moon was nearly full, but there was mist over Wilton Water. Gorse grew thickly on this part of the bank. They halted, peering through prickly boughs. Their breath was like smoke on the cold October air.

'Is she there?' whispered Bethan.

'Hard to tell in this mist.'

'Bet she isn't. My teacher says there's no such thing as a ghost.'

Harry nodded. 'Yeah well, your teacher's never been to look, has she? Loads of people've seen her. Sensible people.'

Bethan shook her head. 'Mum hasn't, and she's lived here for ever.'

Harry sighed. 'Mum refuses to believe in ghosts, full stop. Look.' He pointed.

'Where, *I* can't see anything.'

'See that sapling on the bank over there?'

'Yes.'

'Well, look a little bit to the right of it.'

Bethan peered through the haze, and gasped. A woman in a long black skirt was standing on the water, looking towards the bank.

'You see her *now*, don't you?'

'I see *something*,' croaked Bethan, 'but it looks like it's standing on water. Nobody can stand on water. It's a whatsit illusion.'

'Optical,' whispered Harry. 'But it's *not*, it's the ghost. Me and Rob've seen her five or six times, and she's always exactly the same. If it was an optical illusion, you wouldn't see it twice the same.'

'Why does she stand so still then?'

'How the heck do *I* know, I'm not a ghost.' Harry chuckled. 'If you think it's an optical illusion, why are you whispering, hiding behind a bush? Stand up, give it a shout, see what happens.'

Bethan shook her head. 'No.'

'No, 'cause you *know* it's a ghost. Mum doesn't believe 'cause she doesn't want to. Some people are like that about ghosts.'

Bethan stared at the phantom. She saw a woman pointing a long, pale finger at the water. Try as she might, she couldn't turn it into a tree stump, a twist of vapour or a blend of moonlight and shadow. And she *did* try. After all, thousands of people see something on Loch Ness and mistake it for a monster. *If you expect to see a monster*, she thought, *you see one. And if you expect to see a ghost, you see a ghost.*

'OK,' murmured Harry. 'You wanted to see her, and you have. I better get you home now, or Mum'll make a ghost out of *me*.'

Bethan turned to look back as they moved

3

away. The figure stood as before. *Where does she go in the daytime*, she wondered. *Can she see us? Does she know people come to gawp at her, and does she mind?*

She didn't ask her brother these questions: didn't want to admit she believed, but lying in bed that night it was the ghost she saw when she stared up into the darkness, and when she screwed her eyelids shut the phantom was behind them, keeping her from sleep.

TWO

Sunday morning, Harry's mobi chirped. He freed it from its holster. 'Yep?'

'Rob. Fancy boarding the park for a bit?'

Harry sighed. 'I'm on the net, checking out the Corn Laws. School tomorrow, you know.'

Rob scoffed. ''*Course* I know, that's why I called. Gotta make the most of this last day, man: no more hols till Christmas.'

Harry pulled a face. 'Gotta dash off that assignment for Mottan as well.' Mottan was what the students of Rawton Secondary called the history teacher, whose real name was Bailey.

5

'Haven't you done it yet, you moron? You've had a week.'

'Yeah, but you know how it is. Mum wittering. Kid sister. Stuff to do. I forgot.'

'OK, listen up. Mine's done. I'll bring it to the park, you can work from it tonight.'

'*Copy*, you mean?'

'It's not *copying*, it's research.'

'It wouldn't be my own work.'

'Is the stuff on the net your own work?'

'Well no, but—'

'Sucker, *please*. What's the point of two of us reading the same sites? That's just duplication of effort. Half ten by the rain shelter. Bring your board.'

Wilton Park had no dedicated boarding track, but there were shallow steps, flat-top walls and smooth tarmac paths. The day was cold but dry, and the two friends spent a couple of hours honing their skills, skinning knees and elbows in the process.

It was just before one o'clock when Carl Hopwood appeared with his two hangers-on. At thirteen, Carl was a year older than Rob and Harry, a year ahead at Rawton. He was a big lad

6

with fair, floppy hair and a broad, reddish face.

'Hey,' he cried when he saw the two boarders. 'Look who's here, guys.' He sauntered towards them with his hands in his pockets. 'It's raggy Harry and his poorer sidekick, Rob the slob.'

Harry picked up his board, tucked it under his arm. 'Hi, Carl. We're not looking for any trouble here.' Carl Hopwood was the school bully. Both boys had been victims since primary school, and it was ongoing.

'You're *not*?' sneered Carl in mock surprise. 'Well that's a shame, 'cause we *are*.' He looked at his friends. 'Aren't we, guys?'

Nigel Stocks grinned, Shaun Modley nodded. Carl's dad was rolling in it. Carl was never short of dosh, and he used it to buy the loyalty of creeps like Stocks and Modley.

'We're watching out for scruffs in two-quid trainers and cut-price kit, making the place look untidy,' said Carl, 'and I reckon we've found 'em.' He turned to his companions. '*Seize* 'em, guys,' he ordered.

Rob and Harry fought. They always did, and they always lost. Rob got Modley on the ear with his board, and Harry punched Carl's big face

7

before they were overwhelmed and pinned to the tarmac. Carl looked down at them, dabbing his burst lip with a tissue.

'OK,' he panted, 'we'll have the trainers for a start. And those cheapo boards. Hold 'em still, guys.' The pair struggled, but Stocks and Modley were solid items. Being pinned down by them was like having a hippo on top of you. Carl pulled off Harry's trainers, then Rob's. He straightened up and sniffed them. 'Uuugh, yuk!' He screwed up his face. '*This* is where the stink was coming from.' He dangled them at arm's length by their laces. 'We'll chuck 'em in the lake to cleanse themselves. What d'you say, guys?'

Modley grinned. His ear was turning purple where the board had slammed it. 'Good idea, boss. D'you mean the trainers, or these plonkers?'

Carl smiled. 'Oh, I think *both*, don't you? Bring 'em.'

The boys were hauled to their feet. Their captors grabbed fistfuls of collar in one hand, pants-seat in the other and gave their victims the bums-rush towards the lake. Carl pranced in front with the boards under one arm, swinging the trainers. There were people about, but nobody interfered.

It was a small lake, but big enough. Carl hurled the shoes into the middle, and the boards followed. Rob and Harry struggled, but it was no use. Split almost in two by the grip on their jeans, and with feet only grazing the ground, they were shoved over the edge. They hit the freezing water and thrashed about, spluttering, while their tormentors jeered.

THREE

'What d'you call *this*, Robert Hattersley?' Mr Bailey held up the clear folder by a corner. The papers inside were crinkled and stained, the words on them practically illegible.

Rob coughed. His cheeks were red. 'Sir, I call it my history assignment.' The kids tittered.

'Do you, indeed?' The history teacher silenced the class with a look. 'D'you want to know what *I* call it, laddie?'

'Not really, sir.'

'I didn't think you would, and I'm going to tell you anyway. I call it an ugly wad of papier-mâché. I call it totally unacceptable. I call it, *take this abomination out of my sight and bring me an A-star essay on the Corn Laws at nine tomorrow morning.* What do I call it, Robert Hattersley?'

'Sir, an ugly wad of papier-mâché ... uh ... totally unacc—'

'Yes, all right.' The teacher smiled grimly. 'I think you've got the message. And this time, *don't* do it in the shower.'

Harry hadn't tittered. He knew his turn was coming, and it did. 'Harry Midgley?'

'Sir.'

'*Your* assignment is *not* constructed out of papier-mâché. Neither is it made out of blancmange, black pudding or balsa wood. It is made out of absolutely nothing. In short, it does not exist. Am I right, Mr Midgley?'

'Yessir.'

'Yessir.' The teacher sighed. 'Excuse?'

'Sir, my computer's down.'

'Is it?' murmured Mottan. 'Is it really?'

'Yessir. It's been down over a week.'

'Has it?' The teacher gazed at his pupil. 'Shall I tell you something about computers, laddie? You'll be astounded, I promise.'

'Yes please, sir.' More titters, silenced in the same way.

'When I was your age, way back in the neolithic, computers did not exist. Well – there were a few, but they were as big as this class-room, and none could be accessed by schoolboys. And yet, I managed to produce essays that were so fine, I eventually won a place at college and ended up standing in front of weird life-forms such as yourself.' Mr Bailey smiled. 'I expect you're agog to know how I did it, aren't you, Midgley?'

'Can't wait, sir,' mumbled Harry.

'Books, laddie. I did it with books. Textbooks, encyclopaedias, dictionaries. Books, as found sometimes in public libraries, even today. There's a fine library here in Rawton. It's gradually morphing into an internet café, but books lurk there still, in dark corners. Ever logged on to a book, Harry Midgley?'

'Yessir.'

'Good, aren't they? They don't go down, ever, and there's no spam, except when some barbarian has used a slice as a bookmark. Why not pop down this evening, check out the library?

It's open till eight. Ask somebody to show you where the encyclopaedias are hidden, and look up the Corn Laws. You'll find them under C. Take notes, then hurry home and produce me an essay at least as good as the one I'm looking forward to from your friend Hattersley. All right?'

'Yessir.'

FOUR

'Bummer.' Three thirty. Rob and Harry were dawdling home.

Rob nodded. 'You can say that again, my old mate.'

'Bummer,' obliged Harry.

'It's all right for *you*,' growled Rob. 'You'll be doing it for the first time. I had it finished, thoroughly professional job, till that creepazoid Carl chucked us in the pond.'

Harry shook his head. 'You should never have had it in your jacket, Rob.'

'I brought it for *you*, you parasite.'

Harry nodded. 'I know, but you should've had

it in your backpack. Backpacks're practically waterproof.'

'Are they heck. And anyway, I didn't *bring* my backpack, did I?'

'That's what I'm saying.'

'Huh!' Rob scowled. 'Last time I do *you* a favour, you landless peasant.'

The two parted at the corner of Leaf Street. The Midgleys lived at number eight. Mum and Bethan were in the kitchen when Harry walked in.

Mum smiled. 'Good day at school, love?'

Harry looked at her. 'Did *you* ever have a good day at school, Mum?'

His mother shrugged. 'Depends, doesn't it? Not good compared to lying on a beach in Antigua, sipping a cool drink from a coconut shell while a fit young guy fanned me with a palm leaf. Good, compared to sitting in the dentist's waiting room, listening to the screams coming from the surgery.'

Harry smiled tightly. 'Well, Mum, let's just say mine was closer to the dentist than the beach, all right? What's for tea?'

It was pizza and chips. Harry was smothering his with ketchup when Mum said, 'Have you heard about the reservoir?' He stopped shaking the bottle.

'What about it?'

'They're going to do some work on it. Bring it up to European standard, whatever that means. We got a letter about it, this morning. It'll mean half-emptying it, and there'll be noise for seven months. They apologize in advance.'

Harry shrugged. 'We won't be able to hear it from here, surely?'

Mum shook her head. 'No we won't. Not unless they're going to use dynamite. But people won't be able to walk round it while the work's going on – they're closing the footpath.'

'What about the ghost?' asked Bethan. 'She'll be really upset, won't she?'

Mum looked at her. 'Don't be silly, Bethan. I've told you there *is* no ghost.'

Bethan nodded. 'There *is*, Mum. We saw her last night, didn't we Harry?'

'Hmm ... yeah,' muttered Harry. 'You were supposed to keep quiet about it though – remember?'

'Never mind what Bethan was supposed to do, young man.' Mum sounded seriously irritated. 'You're not supposed to frighten your sister with silly stories, and you're certainly not supposed to take her anywhere near deep water at any time, let alone in the middle of the night.'

'It wasn't the middle of the night, Mum, it was half past eight.'

'Yes,' put in Bethan. 'And I wasn't a *bit* scared, was I, Harry?' *I've been scared ever since though*, she thought but didn't say. *I'm a bit scared now.*

Harry sighed. 'No, Bethan, you weren't scared.' He looked at his mother. 'I don't understand why you get so screwed up whenever one of us mentions the ghost, Mum.'

His mother frowned. 'There *is* no ghost, Harry, and I don't want your sister's head filled with silly tales. People see UFOs, monsters, saints' faces in bits of mouldy bread. Doesn't mean they're actually *there*. Now, d'you think we could stop talking and eat our food before it gets cold?'

FIVE

Harry had lied to Mottan Bailey. His computer wasn't down, so there was no need to bus it into Rawton and check out the library. After tea he went up to his room and switched on the iMac. Rob had said he'd found loads of stuff on the net about the Corn Laws. Waiting for the machine to boot up, Harry thought about something his mother said yesterday, when he came home soaking wet and told her Carl Hopwood was to blame.

'Carl Hopwood's just like his father,' she murmured. 'Too big for his britches, just because Hopwoods used to rule the roost around here. They built a mill you know, back in the nineteenth century. Nearly everybody in Wilton worked for them at one time. They were known as slave-drivers, and I bet they *were*.' She stooped, pushing Harry's clothes in the dryer. 'Mill's long gone, but not the attitude. Councillor Hopwood gets himself elected time after time 'cause people vote him in out of habit. His father was on the Council before him, and his grandfather as well.' She straightened up. 'I expect young Carl'll get elected too, when folks've forgotten he used to chuck smaller kids in the pond.'

I won't forget, thought Harry as he logged on to the Net. *I'd vote for a pig before I'd vote for that Carl, and I bet Rob would too.*

Rob was right: there *was* loads about the Corn Laws, and it was all as boring as Harry had known it would be. *Who sits for hours and hours typing in this garbage?* he wondered.

He called Rob, asked him if he'd used this or that bit of data. It was important they didn't hand in identical essays.

Rob said, 'Word on the street is, they're draining the reservoir.'

'Yes I know,' said Harry. 'Beth thinks it'll upset the ghost.'

Rob laughed. 'It'll spoil her party trick, for sure. Standing on water, I mean. *Anybody* can stand on dry land.'

'Anybody except my dad,' growled Harry. Dad had gone away when Harry was eight. He had a drink problem and Mum had chucked him out. Harry could just remember the poor guy staggering up the path and falling flat on his face in the doorway.

'Yeah, well . . .' Rob never knew what to say when Harry mentioned his dad. 'Catch you tomorrow, mate, Mottan's room.'

'Nine on the dot, Rob, with your essay. And don't carry it past the pond.'

SIX

'Mum?'

'What is it, Harry?' Tuesday tea time. Christa Midgley was busy with mince and lasagna, the children were setting the table.

'Why do people say *as daft as Hettie Daynes*?'

His mother looked at him sharply. 'Who've you heard saying it?'

Harry smiled. 'Lunch time, Rob turned his peas and mashed potato into a smiley face. The supervisor wandered past, said Rob was daft as Hettie Daynes. Who *is* Hettie Daynes, Mum?'

Christa slid the lasagna into the oven. 'Hettie Daynes is an ancestor of ours, Harry. My great,

21

great aunt to be precise. Something bad happened to her and she lost her mind. Took to tearing her clothes and weeping in public. Nobody knew what was causing her such distress. They started referring to her as Daft Hettie, and that's where the expression came from.' She straightened up, closed the oven door. 'It was cruel and stupid to use Hettie's name in that way, but people weren't very PC in Victorian times.'

Harry nodded. 'Wonder they didn't stick her in the loony-bin.'

'We say *psychiatric hospital*, Harry,' retorted Christa tartly, 'not loony-bin. And no, they didn't lock her up. She disappeared, never to be seen again. Anyway.' She glanced at the clock. 'Tea's in forty-five minutes: just enough time to do your homework.'

Flipping homework, mumbled Harry as he trailed upstairs. *Up till eleven last night for Mottan, and at it again the minute I walk in the door*. At least it was English this time, not history.

He'd been all right this morning though, old Mottan.

'Ah – a *dry* one,' he exclaimed when Rob handed over his assignment.

'Yessir,' Rob joked. 'You see, I *had* my annual shower Sunday night.' It was risky, but the teacher just laughed.

Receiving Harry's folder he asked, 'You found the library then, young Midgley?'

Harry shook his head. 'No need, sir, my computer decided to work.'

Mottan treated him to a wry smile. 'Perhaps you'll take the same decision yourself, laddie.' Probably a decent bloke really, Mottan.

Can't say the same for Carl Hopwood though. He approached the pair at morning break. 'Wise of you not to grass me up,' he purred. 'I get quite irritated when somebody splits on me, and my associates don't like it either.' He smiled nastily. 'Get on the wrong side of a Hopwood and you'll find yourself in deep water.' He forced a laugh. '*Deep water* – geddit?'

Prat.

SEVEN

It's dark after tea in October, and Bethan wasn't allowed out after dark. Trouble was, she couldn't stop thinking about the ghost.

No such thing according to Mum, but she'd seen it. A woman in a long skirt. If Bethan stared up at the ceiling when she was lying in the dark, the woman always appeared, standing in the middle of the floating shapes and phantom lights you always see when you do that. Even with her eyes screwed shut she'd see her for a while, till she'd slowly lose shape and melt to a blob.

Bethan didn't see the ghost in the daytime, but

it was inside her head and Bethan couldn't get rid of it. It was interfering with her work in class. *I've got to see her again*, she thought. *If I can just get one more look, perhaps I'll be able to stop thinking about her.*

At break time she talked to her best friend, Alison. Alison's mum wasn't strict, Alison got away with all sorts of stuff. Sometimes her mum let Alison have a friend to sleep over, even when it wasn't her birthday or anything.

'Hey, Aly,' said Bethan. 'D'you want to see the ghost?'

'What ghost?'

'The ghost of Wilton Water of course.'

Alison shook her head. 'Don't believe in her.'

'Well neither did I, till Harry took me to see her.'

'You *saw* her?'

'Yes, and now I can't stop thinking about her.'

Alison laughed. 'You mean she's *haunting* you?'

Bethan nodded. 'In a way, yes. I need to see her again, then maybe she'll leave me alone.'

'So why me? Too scared to go by yourself, is that it?'

'No, but I'm not allowed out after dark. I was wondering . . . ?'

'What?'

'Well, if I could sleep over at yours, say on Saturday? We could go up the reservoir after tea. Your mum wouldn't mind, would she?'

"Course not,' smiled Alison. 'And I wouldn't mind checking out this so-called ghost myself. I'll ask Mum and give you a ring, OK?'

'Magic.'

Alison shook her head. 'No magic, no ghost, but we'll have a laugh. See ya.'

EIGHT

'*Big Issue,* sir?' said the thin man to the beefy one in a blue suit.

It was Thursday lunch time, and Councillor Reginald Hopwood was on his way to The Feathers for his customary plate of something and a pint. He didn't break his stride, dashing aside the thin man's magazine with a dimpled hand. 'Get a job,' he snarled, 'instead of hanging around begging, making the place look untidy.'

'This *is* my job,' protested the thin man to the councillor's receding back. 'I'm an official vendor.'

'Official scrounger, you mean,' growled

Hopwood as he strode away. He was a busy man, and a hungry one. The vendor gazed after him for a moment, then shrugged and turned away.

The pub was busy too. The landlord looked up as Hopwood shouldered his way through the crowd.

'Afternoon, Councillor!' he boomed. Reginald liked to be called Councillor, especially where a lot of people could hear. 'The usual?'

Hopwood nodded. It pleased him that the landlord knew what he always drank. It showed he was a valued customer.

He carried his pint of bitter to the corner table the landlord reserved for him every Thursday. He sat down and sipped his beer, watching the door. A minute or two later Stan Fox came through it.

'Now then, Councillor.' Fox slipped into his customary seat and grinned at Hopwood across the table. 'Anything I should know?' Stan Fox was senior reporter on the *Rawton Echo*, the town's weekly newspaper. Hopwood kept him informed about council business, and Fox made sure the councillor's name and picture graced the front page from time to time.

Hopwood smiled. 'We've decided who'll do the reservoir job.'

The reporter looked at him. 'Who?'

'Forgan.'

Fox frowned. 'But I thought it was going to be Wexley.'

The councillor nodded. 'It was, but Forgan came up with an offer we couldn't refuse.'

'What offer?'

'Playground for the school, state of the art, no charge.' Hopwood shrugged. 'Rude to say no.'

The reporter grinned. 'And for you?'

'How d'you mean, for me?'

'I mean for you personally, Reginald. You had to approve Forgan. What did they give you?'

'Well.' Hopwood winked, rubbed the side of his nose with a finger. 'Expenses, you know? The usual out of pocket expenses.' He looked at the reporter. 'That's off the record, of course.'

'Of course.' Fox raised his glass. 'To you, Councillor.' He grinned. 'I assume lunch is on you?'

'Naturally,' purred Hopwood.

NINE

Thursday, after tea. Christa Midgley riffled through a sheaf of bills on the table while Harry and Bethan did the washing up.

'Mum?'

'What is it, Bethan?' She tried to keep the irritation out of her voice, but she was tired. Tired after her long day working down the minimarket: tired of the endless struggle to make ends meet.

'Can I sleep over at Alison's, Saturday night?'

Her mother sighed. 'Why, is there a party or something? It isn't Alison's birthday again *already*, surely?'

Bethan giggled. 'No, Mum, she only has one a year, in May. This is a sleepover for no special reason, it'll just be her and me. Can I, Mum, *pleeeease?*'

Christa scribbled something on the bottom of the gas bill, looked up. 'Has Alison asked her mother if it's all right to invite you?'

''Course. She's the coolest mum in Wilton, Mrs Crabtree. Lets Alison do just about anything she wants. Probably won't even notice I'm there.'

Christa shook her head. 'No, and that's what worries me, Bethan. I was at school with Norah Crabtree, and she was just the same then. Didn't let anything get to her. She'd come to school looking like a trainee bag lady, and sit gawping out of the window all day. She wasn't Crabtree then of course, she was Nolan. Anyway, I can never quite relax while you're at Alison's, sweetheart.'

'Oh, Mu-um!' Bethan stood with a plate in one hand and a tea towel in the other, looking tragic. Harry came up behind her and squeezed out the dishcloth over her head. She shrieked, turned and swiped at him with the tea towel. The plate

31

slipped out of her hand and shattered on the tiles. Bethan burst into tears.

It came right in the end. Harry was sent to his room till bedtime, no TV. The pieces of plate were picked up, binned and forgotten. Bethan got a hug, and her mum relented.

Ghost-watch was go.

TEN

At morning break Friday, Rob and Harry strolled round the perimeter of the all-weather pitch. It was a still, warm day, with a thin haze that hinted it might be one of the last.

'There's a ginormous digger by the reservoir,' said Rob. Wilton Water was just about visible from his house.

'Yeah?' Harry kicked a pebble. 'It's starting then. We should check it out, home time.'

Rob shrugged. 'Sure, why not.'

The day dragged. Fridays always drag, like the weekend's dug its heels in, doesn't want to come.

The saying *time marches on* should have a bit added to it that says: *except at school*.

Three thirty came at last, and the two friends headed for Wilton and the reservoir, wading through drifts of fallen leaves. On the banks of Wilton Water gorse still flowered, though sparsely. The light was fading, but the booms of two earth-movers stood silhouetted against the sky at the western end, where the overflow lay.

'Look like dinosaurs don't they?' said Rob.

'Uh . . . oh, yeah.' Harry was gazing where he and Bethan had seen the ghost. The water there lay black and still, no figure stood on its surface. He shivered though, and cried out when some-body emerged from a nearby clump of alder.

Rob laughed at his friend. 'What's *up*, you numpty, it's only Steve.'

'Steve?' croaked Harry. 'Who the heck's . . . ?'

'Steve Wood. You know – local history guy. Writes books, gives talks to schools?'

'Oh. Oh yeah. *That* Steve.' His heart was still pounding.

Steve Wood approached. Tall, thin, long-haired, he regarded the boys through wire-rimmed grandad glasses. 'Hi. They're part draining this, y'know. Should see stuff that's not been seen since it filled up in eighteen eighty-five.'

'Like what?' asked Rob.

'There were two farms and a mill in this little valley,' Steve told him. 'They'll still be here – traces of them I mean. I'm interested in Hopwood Mill. It should be just over there.'

'*Hopwood* Mill?' Harry looked at the historian. 'Hopwood, as in *Councillor* Hopwood and Carl, his tunnel-dwarf son?'

Wood nodded. 'Oh yes. The councillor's ancestor, Josiah Hopwood, built the mill in eighteen o nine. It was a cotton mill. Practically everybody in the village worked there in Victorian times. It made Josiah rich. He had Hopwood House built, where the family still lives.' He smiled. 'Some say the mill was starting to fail in the eighteen eighties, and the water company came along at the perfect moment and bought it. Some old villagers still talk about the Hopwood luck.'

Harry looked where the historian had pointed. 'And you think they'll take enough water out so the mill will be on dry land?'

Steve chuckled. 'I don't know about *dry*. My guess is it'll be seriously muddy, but it should be possible to get close to whatever's left wearing wellies. Or barefoot, if you like the squish of mud between your toes.'

'I think I'll pass,' growled Rob. 'Go for the wellies.'

Harry nodded. 'Me too. When d'you think it'll be, Steve?'

The historian shook his head. 'No idea. You'd have to ask the contractors, only I wouldn't if I were you; I suspect they'll want to keep locals well away from the place till the work's finished. Anyway.' He stretched, yawned. 'I'm off for my tea now. I'll probably see you around.'

The two boys watched him stride away. 'Seems a nice enough guy,' said Harry, 'for a gravedodger.'

Rob nodded. 'He's the star of my dad's quiz team at The Lamb.'

'Ah.' Harry's dad had been a sort of star at The Lamb, but it had nothing to do with the quiz team and Harry didn't want to think about it. 'I'm ready for a spot of tea myself,' he chirped. 'Come on.'

ELEVEN

'What's it like?' asked Bethan. It was half past five. The Midgleys were eating sausages and mash.

Harry shrugged. 'Doesn't look any different yet, apart from the diggers.' He looked at his mother. 'We met Steve Wood, d'you know him?'

Christa nodded. 'I know *of* him, Harry. He was a postman, years ago. He's into local history now – does research at Rawton Library, writes books. The *Echo* prints his articles now and again. I expect he's looking forward to the water level dropping – it'll uncover lots of local history.'

Harry nodded. 'There's a mill, Mum.

Hopwood Mill. Steve says Carl's ancestor built it – Josiah Hopwood.'

His mother nodded. 'That's right. Most of *our* ancestors worked there. My great, great auntie started when she was ten.'

'*Ten?*'

'Yes, it was quite usual in those days. They started very early in the morning, too.' She smiled. 'They worked three hours before the Hopwood children got out of bed.'

'What about school?' asked Bethan.

'Lots of children left school at ten, love. Some never went at all.'

'Huh – lucky them. *I'm* ten. Wish *I* could leave.'

Her mother shook her head. 'They weren't lucky, Bethan. Just think: trudging through snow at half past five on a winter morning. No breakfast, no warm clothes, clogs on your feet. And all for a shilling or two a week.'

'What's a shilling?'

Christa smiled. 'Well, it's five pence now, but it was worth more in those days. You could probably buy . . . oh . . . six loaves of bread and a packet of tea for a shilling.'

'They worked all week for bread and tea?'

Her mother nodded. 'And beef fat, perhaps. That's what they'd have on their bread, instead of butter.'

Bethan pulled a face. 'Ugh!'

'Yes – ugh! So you see, *we're* the lucky ones. My great, great auntie never tasted pizza, never had ice cream, never saw the sea. So.' She smiled. 'Let's get these plates to the sink, break out the ice cream and be thankful the mill's been underwater all our lives.'

TWELVE

Alison had three big brothers, so there was no spare bedroom at the Crabtrees' house. Bethan got to share Alison's room so the pair could talk half the night.

Bethan liked the family's way with time. Mostly, they ignored it. There was no such thing as breakfast time, lunch time, tea time or bedtime. When somebody got hungry, he stuck something in the microwave and ate it in front of the telly, which was never switched off. The table was used only to pile stuff on: clothes, cassettes, magazines, junk mail. You went to bed when you were tired, and at weekends got up when you felt like it. The only clock in the house was on the DVD player. It didn't work, and nobody cared.

Bethan arrived at four o'clock Saturday afternoon. In her backpack were her phone, some favourite CDs, her mum's digital camera, a change of underwear and her pyjamas. Mr Crabtree and the three boys were out watching Rawton Rovers play Darlington. Mrs Crabtree and Alison were watching an ancient movie on TV.

'Come on in, lovey,' smiled Alison's mum. 'Sit down, make yourself at home, I'll put the kettle on in a bit.'

She didn't. They watched the movie. When it was over, Mrs Crabtree switched channels.

Alison got up. 'Come on,' she said to Bethan, 'there's burgers in the fridge, we can have 'em with crisps and coke.'

They carried the meal up to Alison's room.

'We don't want to be downstairs when Dad and the boys get back,' said Alison. 'If Rovers've lost they'll be as miserable as sin, and if they've won they'll be as daft as Hettie Daynes.'

'D'you know who Hettie Daynes *was*?' asked Bethan, as they settled on the bed with their plates.

41

Alison shook her head. 'Haven't the faintest. It's an expression my gran uses, that's all I know.'

'She was our ancestor, lived here in Wilton about a hundred years ago. Went barmy, then vanished. My mum told me.'

'Wow! Never thought of her as a real person. Hey.' Alison grinned. 'Maybe the reservoir ghost's Hettie Daynes.'

Bethan shook her head. 'I don't think so. People'd *call* it Hettie Daynes if it were, wouldn't they?'

They ate the crisps and burgers, drank the coke. Presently, the family car came growling along the pathway under Alison's window. Her brothers piled out. The girls peered down. 'They lost,' declared Alison. 'They'd be making more row otherwise.'

'Could've been a draw,' suggested Bethan.

Her friend shrugged. 'Maybe. Anyway,' she grinned, 'who gives a stuff?'

They stayed where they were while the menfolk stamped and bashed about downstairs, getting their tea. Beyond the window, twilight deepened.

'What time we going?' murmured Bethan.

'What time *is* it?' asked Alison.

Bethan looked at her watch. 'Coming up to six.'

'We can set off now if you like.'

They went down to the hallway, got their jackets. Bethan slipped the camera into a pocket. Alison popped her head round the kitchen door. 'Off up the reservoir, Dad, OK?'

'All right, love,' said Mr Crabtree. One of the boys growled, 'If you see any Darlington fans up there, shove 'em in.'

They left the house and strolled towards the haunted water.

THIRTEEN

'Hey look – they've started draining it.' Bethan pointed to the water line. It had fallen quite a bit, leaving the reservoir's fringe of reeds high and dry. It was dark, but the two girls could just make out the shapes of diggers and dumpers up at the western end. As far as they could tell, they had Wilton Water to themselves.

'Where's this famous ghost then?' mocked Alison. 'I didn't invite you to sleep over so we could gawp at a few diggers.'

'She's over there.' Bethan nodded towards the place she and Harry had seen the apparition.

44

Alison strained her eyes. 'Where? I don't see anything.'

Bethan shook her head. 'No, I mean that's where she stands when she's here. She's not there at the moment.'

'Ha!' scoffed Alison. 'You'll be telling me next she's popped down to the Co-op for a loaf, back in a couple of minutes.'

'Don't talk daft,' snapped Bethan. 'We'll get a bit closer, behind those gorse bushes, OK?'

Alison shrugged. 'Then what?'

'We wait and watch.'

'Huh!'

They crouched by the gorse, watching the water. There was no wind, but something was rippling the surface, the ripples reflecting sparks of light that had no apparent source. The only sounds were muffled ones, of traffic far away.

Alison sighed, fidgeted. 'Told you,' she murmured. 'There's no flipping ghost. I'm off.'

'No, Aly, don't go.' Bethan clutched her friend's sleeve. 'Give it one more minute.'

Alison subsided. 'OK, Bethan, one minute. *One.*' She gazed at the only visible star, counting seconds in her head.

Bethan gnawed her bottom lip and stared into the dark.

She was there. Hard to pick out against the trees, but *there*. Probably been there all the time.

Bethan touched Alison's sleeve, pointed. 'There, *look.*'

Alison's eyes followed the trembling finger. She started to shake her head, then gasped. 'Yeah, there *is* something . . . a shape . . . *does* look like . . . crikey!'

Bethan eased the camera out of her pocket.

Alison plucked at her jacket, whispered, 'What you doing? Don't leave me.'

''S OK.' Bethan touched her friend's hair. 'Need to get a shot, see – proof.'

Alison stared at the motionless wraith, so like the black trunks behind it. *It's a tree*, she told herself. *Just a tree, except* . . . That pale smudge, just where you'd expect a face to be. And another one, smaller, farther down. A *hand*?

The flash made her jump. A brief whirr, and Bethan was back beside her, brandishing the camera. '*Got* her!' she hissed. 'Right in the middle of the frame. Is she still there?'

Alison peered through narrowed eyes. The

flash had left a greenish, floating blob. She looked past it. The figure, if it was a figure, hadn't moved. She nodded. 'Yeah, still there.'

'Unbelievable.' Bethan shook her head. 'I thought that flash . . .'

'Can we go now, Bethan?' Alison's voice sounded hoarse. 'I don't feel too good.'

'Yes, sure, come on.' Bethan slid a hand under her friend's arm and they started back the way they'd come. Bethan glanced behind, but the gorse was in the way.

You're real though, she said inside her head. *I've got a pic, and a witness.* She pressed quick view, thrust the camera under Alison's nose.

'See – I'm not barmy, am I?'

Alison shook her head and shivered. 'Wish you *were*,' she murmured.

FOURTEEN

Norah Crabtree peered at her daughter in the light from the TV. 'What's up, lovey – somebody bother you or something?'

'No.' Alison shook her head. 'Nothing's up, Mum, honest. Where's Dad?'

Her mother snorted. 'Guess.'

'Down The Lamb?'

'Right first time. And the lads're out somewhere, don't ask.' She frowned. '*Something*'s shaken you up, Aly, I can tell.' She turned to Bethan. 'What is it, Bethan – what happened?'

Bethan looked down. 'It's nothing really, Mrs

48

Crabtree. We . . . we saw the ghost. I don't think Alison believed in her.'

'Ghost?' Norah Crabtree laughed. 'Ghost, my foot.' She looked at Alison. 'I've told you before, you great softie, there's no such thing as a ghost.' She sighed. 'There's enough to worry about in the real world without making stuff up to scare yourself with.'

Alison looked at her mother. 'Bethan got a picture.'

Norah turned to Bethan. 'Picture?'

Bethan produced the camera. 'Yes, Mrs Crabtree. On this.'

'You've got a photo of a *ghost*?' Norah held out her hand. 'Let me see.'

Bethan pulled a face. 'I haven't really looked myself yet, it might be a bit . . .' She pressed quick view, peered at the screen. 'Yeah,' she murmured, 'it's not very sharp.'

'Give it here.' Norah zapped the TV, plunging the room into darkness. 'If there's a ghost I'll see it, and that'll be a first.'

Bethan passed her the camera.

There was a long silence while Norah stared at the tiny screen. She tilted the camera, rotated it, held it close to her eyes and far away. The two girls watched. After a while she cleared her throat and murmured, 'There's something that *could* be a person, but it must be a stump, a shadow, a trick of the light.' She handed the camera back to Bethan. 'People have come up with photos of flying saucers, lovey. Fairies. The Loch Ness Monster.' She chuckled. 'A newspaper even printed a picture of an old aeroplane they reckoned had crashed on the *moon*.' She shook her head. 'All sorts of funny things happen with photos. I'd whatsit if I were you, Bethan – delete it.'

Bethan shook her head. 'I think I'd like to look at it on a computer screen first, Mrs Crabtree, if you don't mind.'

Norah shrugged. 'I don't mind, lovey, 'course not – it's *your* camera.' She smiled. 'Just don't go having nightmares about it, that's all – either of you.'

FIFTEEN

This was Bethan's nightmare. It was night. She stood on the shore of Wilton Water, alone. There was a brilliant moon. Everything stood out clearly – no blurring of one object into another.

The woman's face, silvery like the moon, was turned towards her. One thin white hand was visible against the black skirt. The index finger pointed down.

Bethan looked where the finger pointed, then at the luminous face. The spectre stood motionless, its eyes pools of inky shadow. It didn't speak or beckon, yet Bethan felt herself called.

She was moving down the bank. Reeds

51

brushed her bare legs. Water spilled into her shoes, so cold it made her cry out. She called to the spectre: I'm not like you, I have weight, the water won't . . .

It was then she heard Mrs Crabtree say, *I'd whatsit if I were you, Bethan – delete it.*

The water was up to her knees. She woke.

'Wakey wakey, Bethan.' Alison was shaking her. 'Put a sock in it, you numpty, you'll have everyone out of bed.'

'I have weight,' mumbled Bethan, 'the water won't support me.'

'Yeah, whatever.' Alison giggled. 'You've been yelling the place down, what happened?'

'Huh?' Bethan shook her head to disperse the last shreds of dream. 'Oh . . . she called me, Aly. I tried to walk to her, but I was sinking. Then I heard your mum.'

'Yeah,' Alison nodded, 'and Mum heard *you*, I bet.' She smiled. 'Anyway it was a dream.' Her smile faded. 'Last night though – we did see her, didn't we? *That* wasn't a dream.'

'No,' murmured Bethan, 'that was a *nightmare*, Aly.' She shivered. 'One I wish I could wake from.'

SIXTEEN

Sunday morning, half past eight. Bethan lay on her side, looking across the room at the sleeping Alison. She'd slept like a log herself after the scary dream.

Come on, Aly, she thought, *wake up – we've stuff to do*. They'd decided to link the camera to Alison's iMac, get the snapshot on the big screen. If the ghost showed up clearer, Aly would call her mum to come and look.

Bethan was impatient to begin, but there was no way you could rush this family. The expression *laid back* might have been invented for the Crabtrees. She rolled onto her back, clasped her hands under her head and closed her eyes.

She must have fallen asleep, because the next thing she knew Alison was shaking her. 'Come on, lazybones, let's not waste the day.'

'Uh?' Bethan scowled at her friend. 'What a cheek! I was awake ages before you, must've nodded off again.'

'Yeah, right,' growled Alison. 'There's a bacon butty on the unit, and a coffee.'

Alison dressed while Bethan ate, then booted up the computer. 'I can't actually do the photo bit myself,' she admitted. 'Have to get our Tony to do it.'

One by one, the Crabtrees rose to fix their various breakfasts. Seventeen-year-old Tony carried his banana and marmalade sandwich into his sister's room. 'What you got that's so desperately urgent you have to get a guy up in the middle of the night?' he grumbled.

'Middle of the *night*?' Alison laughed. 'It's quarter to ten, you skulking loafer.'

The lad shook his tousled head. 'Yeah, but it's *Sunday*, sweetheart. What *have* you got?'

'Ghost,' said Alison. 'On Wilton Water.'

'Wilton *backside*,' growled her brother.

Alison nodded. 'That's what Mum said, more or less.'

Both girls secretly hoped the enlarged snapshot would show only stumps and shadows. Ghosts are exciting as an idea, but nobody really wants to be involved with one.

It was there though, plain as Bethan's nightmare. Same moon-washed face, same pools of shadow hiding the eyes, same pointing finger.

'Blooming heck!' spluttered Tony, stippling the screen with bits of sandwich.

Norah Crabtree arrived in her dressing gown. She peered over Tony's shoulder, made a little choking sound in her throat.

'I can enhance it,' he offered.

'D . . . don't bother,' croaked his mother. 'It's bad enough the way it is.' She shivered, pulling the dressing gown more snugly round her. 'Hang on while I fetch Dad.'

Mr Crabtree declared himself flabbergasted. 'I never believed,' he murmured. 'Thought it was a load of old cobblers in fact.' He looked at Bethan. 'How about I phone the *Echo*, sweetheart – make you famous?'

'Oh, I don't know, Mr Crabtree,' protested Bethan, but she was too late. He was already on his mobi.

SEVENTEEN

Luckily for Bethan, the newsroom of the *Rawton Echo* had only one man on duty Sundays. He listened to Mr Crabtree's story and said, 'I'll run it by Stan Fox, sir, first thing tomorrow morning. He's our senior reporter, he'll decide whether to send somebody round. What's the address again?'

'Coming tomorrow,' said Mr Crabtree, pocketing his mobi. 'Perhaps.' He looked at Tony. 'Better save it, son.' He turned to Bethan. 'Can you get round here in the morning, sweetheart? They'll want to talk to the photographer in person.'

Bethan shook her head. 'It's school, Mr Crabtree, I can't.'

'Can't you bunk off, just for one morning?' He sounded really disappointed. 'It's not every day you get the chance to be famous, you know.'

Bethan pulled a face. 'My mum wouldn't let me. And anyway, I can't let her find out I was at the reservoir after dark, she'd kill me.' She looked at Tony. 'Can't you say *you* took the picture, Tony?'

The lad nodded. 'I could, I suppose, but then I'd get famous instead of you.'

Bethan nodded. 'That's all right, I don't mind.'

Mr Crabtree shook his head. 'Won't work, sweetheart. I told the guy my daughter's friend took it.'

'Oh, heck,' groaned Bethan.

'*I* know,' beamed Mr Crabtree. 'I'll say *I* was with you and Aly. Your mum wouldn't mind you going to the reservoir with your friend's dad, would she?'

Bethan shrugged, stared at the floor. She suspected her mother's distrust of Norah Crabtree extended to the man she'd married, but you just can't say that sort of thing. Instead she mumbled, 'I never said I wanted it in the paper, Mr Crabtree. I wish you'd call back and say it was a mistake or a joke or something.'

Mr Crabtree was about to protest when his wife chipped in. 'If that's what Bethan wants, Gilbert, you'd best do it. It's her snapshot after all.'

'Hmmm.' Mr Crabtree frowned, looked at Bethan. 'If you're sure, sweetheart?'

Bethan nodded. 'Yes please, Mr Crabtree.'

A reluctant Mr Crabtree made the call, and not long afterwards Bethan left her friend's house and set off home. She knew she'd disappointed him, but he ought not to have phoned the paper without giving her the chance to object. *I didn't want to be famous*, she told herself. *All I wanted was to see the ghost again, so I could maybe stop thinking about her all the time.*

Hasn't worked though, 'cause she's still here, doing my head in. Wish, wish, wish I could get her out of my head . . .

EIGHTEEN

Christa was dusting the living room. She paused as Bethan walked in. 'Hello, love, did you have a good time?'

Bethan nodded. 'Yes, Mum, thanks. We played music till late. It was cool.'

'Crabtrees all well?'

Bethan shrugged. 'Far as I know. Where's Harry?'

'In his room, I expect, glued to that computer.'

Bethan nodded. 'I'll take my stuff up, see you in a bit.'

Her brother looked up as she stuck her head round his door. 'Go to i-photo,' she hissed, 'I've something to show you.' She dropped her pack in her own room, returned with the camera.

'Wow!' Harry gazed at the screen. 'It's her all right, Sis. How the heck . . . ?'

'Ssssh!' Bethan glanced towards the door. 'Don't let Mum hear. Me and Aly went up the res last night, she'd kill me if she knew.'

Her brother nodded. 'OK, only this is *fantastic*, Sis, yeah? I mean, I don't think anybody's ever managed to snap a ghost before: not even those paranormal investigators with all their fancy paraphernalia. We've got to let someone see this because it's . . . well, it's *historic*.'

Bethan shook her head. 'No, Harry, we *can't*. I told you Mum'd kill me, and anyway I had this dream.' Briefly, she described her nightmare. 'I think she *wants* something, Harry.'

The boy grunted. 'Like *what*, Sis?'

'Well *I* don't know, do I? She was like this.' Bethan pointed a rigid finger at the carpet. 'Aly thinks it's Hettie Daynes, and Mum says Hettie disappeared so it makes sense.' She gripped her brother's arm. 'I want us to investigate, Harry. We're always looking for adventure and never finding any, and now we've found it.' She looked

61

into his eyes. 'Please, Harry, let's keep it to ourselves and investigate.'

Harry gazed at the screen for half a minute, then nodded. 'OK, Sis, we'll give it a whirl. But I'm saving this, and if we don't find anything out, we show it to somebody. All right?'

Bethan nodded. 'Yes, all right.'

NINETEEN

'Forgan?' Councillor Hopwood was on his mobi. 'Hopwood here. We met at Rawton Town Hall.'

'I remember. How are you, Councillor?'

'I'm fine. Listen. This Wilton Water job.'

'Yes: nothing wrong I hope?'

'Not so far, but the Council's worried about public safety.'

'I can assure you, Councillor Hopwood, my company's safety record is among the very best in the industry.'

'I know, Forgan, I know. I've read the literature. It's just . . . well, I know Wilton people. I should:

63

most of 'em worked for my family at one time. They're stubborn, and they're nosy. I've seen the Keep Out signs you've put up, and I can tell you they won't work. The minute there's anything to see, folk'll be swarming everywhere, gawping. Especially the kids. The Council wants to see barriers, Forgan. If somebody drowns, it won't only be the water company that gets sued, it'll be us. We think you ought to keep a watchman on site as well.'

'We don't employ watchmen, Councillor. We've never found it necessary. Warning notices, plastic tape. They work.'

'Barriers, Forgan. I've some influence with the water company, I don't want to have to tell 'em we've no confidence in you.'

'There'll be no need for that, Councillor. If you insist, I'll see you have barriers, and I'll get back to you on the watchman thing.'

'D'you know Forgan, I *knew* you'd understand. Goodbye.'

TWENTY

'You got a *picture*?' gasped Rob. It was Monday morning, just before the bell.

Harry nodded. 'Bethan did. It's in her camera.'

'Crikey! What's she gonna do with it?'

Harry shrugged. 'She wants to investigate. Reckons the ghost is trying to tell us something. Her mate Alison thinks it's Hettie Daynes.'

Rob frowned. 'Who *is* this Hettie Daynes? Name keeps cropping up, never heard of her.'

Harry had just outlined the story his mother had told when the bell rang. 'Later,' said Rob. They joined the kids crowding into school. Registration was barely over when a note came round from the Head. Hezzy, real name Miss Tate, cleared her throat to get the year's attention.

'Note from Mr Woollard. It concerns us all, but particularly those of you who live in Wilton, because it's about Wilton Water.' She scanned the single sheet. 'Apparently the reservoir is undergoing renovation, and the powers that be are concerned that people might be tempted to go sightseeing there while work is in progress. Mr Woollard points out that this could be highly dangerous, and expects all students of this school to stay well clear throughout the four months it will take to complete the project.' She folded the note, handed it back to the kid who brought it, scanned the class. 'Is that quite clear to you all?'

It was. Harry would be sightseeing regardless, but he grunted and nodded like everybody else. The Head's reputation as a disciplinarian had earned him the nickname 'Well 'ard', but he lived a long way from Wilton Water. If a couple of kids went roaming its shores on dark winter evenings or foggy Saturday afternoons, how the heck was he going to know?

TWENTY-ONE

As Miss Tate was reading out the Head's note at Rawton Secondary, Bethan's teacher clapped for attention at Wilton Primary. 'Listen, everybody.' The hum of voices faded, all eyes were on Miss Newbould.

'Hallowe'en is a week on Friday. That's only twelve days away, so it's time to start thinking about our costumes for the Hallowe'en Hop. There's to be a competition, with a valuable prize for the most original outfit.' The teacher paused, then went on. 'Remember, I said the *most original*. You're not likely to win if you come as a witch or a wizard or a skeleton or a vampire, because

67

that's what most people tend to come as.' She
smiled. 'The challenge is to think up something a
bit different. Our Chair of Governors will be
judging the competition, and that's what he'll
be looking for.'

'Miss?' Alison Crabtree raised her hand.

'Yes, Alison?'

'Miss, is it all right if I come as—'

'Whoa!' Miss Newbould broke in. 'Don't *tell*
us, Alison, or somebody might copy your idea.
Keep it to yourself, ask your mum to help with
the sewing, surprise us all on the night. All right?'

'Yes, miss.'

Morning break. Bethan and Alison strolled
round the edge of the playing field, talking.
Bethan looked at her friend.

'So what's this brilliant idea for a costume, Aly?
I won't copy, honest.'

Alison smiled. 'I know you won't, silly.' She put
her lips near Bethan's ear and whispered, though
nobody was close. 'Hettie Daynes.'

'Hey, *brilliant*!' Bethan grinned. 'You know
Hettie's an ancestor of ours, of course. Mum says
she used to tear her clothes. You could get a long
skirt from the charity shop and rip great holes in

it. You could mess up your hair and put muck on your face. And *I* know – you could come barefoot, that's *dead* original.'

Alison nodded. 'I know. You don't mind, do you? With her being an ancestor, I mean?'

Bethan shook her head. 'Course not. I'll mention it to Mum, but I'm sure it'll be all right.' She smiled. 'At least you won't need to practise looking barmy, Aly – you do already.'

She skipped sideways to avoid a slap.

TWENTY-TWO

Monday, five fifteen. The Midgleys round the table, eating spaghetti and meatballs in tomato sauce. Bethan looked across at her mother. 'Mum?'

'Yes, love?'

'You know the Hallowe'en Hop?'

Christa nodded. 'I know *of* it, yes. Week on Friday. You'll need a costume of some sort.'

'Yes, only I haven't decided what to go as.'

Her mother smiled. 'Isn't that what the Americans call a no-brainer, sweetheart? I mean, girls go as witches, right?'

'Well yes, Mum, but you see it's a competition,

to see who can come up with the most original costume. A witch outfit might be original at somebody's *wedding*, but not at a Hallowe'en Hop.' She pulled a face. 'There's a totally awesome one, but Aly bagged it.'

'Alison *Crabtree*?' Christa sounded surprised.

Beth nodded. 'Yes, she's going as Hettie Daynes.'

Christa set down her fork and whispered, 'She's going as *who*?'

'H . . . Hettie Daynes.' Bethan could tell by her mother's expression, the softness of her voice, that this had not gone down well. She gulped. 'What's up, Mum?'

Christa gazed at her daughter, spoke softly. 'What's up, Bethan? You *know* what's up. I told you Hettie Daynes was my great, great auntie. She was an actual person, not somebody out of a silly tale. She lived here in Wilton, just like you and me. Something terrible happened to her, and she lost her mind. She wasn't something to *dress up* as, in the hope of winning a competition. It's like dressing up as one of those poor starving toddlers in Africa, or somebody who's been maimed by a bomb. You just don't *do* that

71

sort of thing, Bethan. It's ... it's in bad taste.'

'But, Mum ...' Bethan looked stricken. 'Aly was so excited when she told me – how can I tell her she's got to forget the whole thing?'

Her mother shook her head. 'You must just *tell* her, Bethan. Unless you'd rather *I* told her.'

'Uh ... no thanks, Mum – I'll see to it.'

TWENTY-THREE

First thing Tuesday morning, Bethan found her friend in the yard. 'Hi, Aly.'

'Hi yourself.' Alison studied Bethan's face. 'What's up – you look like you lost a solid gold bangle or something.'

Bethan sighed. 'It's worse than that. Listen. I've something to tell you, and a favour to ask.'

'Go on.'

Bethan told her friend what happened yesterday tea time. When she'd finished, Aly said, 'Oh heck – I can see why your mum's upset. You're going to ask me to drop the idea, aren't you?'

'No.' Bethan shook her head. 'I was awake half the night thinking, and you won't need to drop it – just change it a bit.'

'Change it *how*?'

'Well, you think the *ghost* is Hettie, don't you?'

'Ye-es.'

'So don't go as Hettie Daynes, just go as the ghost.'

'That'll make a difference?'

''*Course* it will. Mum doesn't believe in the ghost – says it's only a tale, so if you go as the ghost she'll have no objection.' She gazed at her friend. 'Do it, Aly – for me. It'll still be original.'

Alison was quiet for a moment, then she nodded. 'Yes, OK.' She pulled a face. 'I'll need a long black skirt instead of a torn one, and lots of white make-up instead of dirt.' She grinned. 'I'll be like a Goth. And I'll stand pointing down like she does. It'll be *dead* dramatic.'

Tea time, Bethan said, 'Mum, I talked to Aly. She's changed her mind, she won't go as Hettie Daynes. She's going as the ghost of Wilton Water.'

Christa nodded. 'That's much better, Bethan. And what about you – what will *you* go as?'

Harry grinned. 'She could go as *herself*, Mum – scare everyone to death.'

'Yes,' snapped Bethan, 'or I could go as *you* – I don't think anyone's been as the village idiot before.'

TWENTY-FOUR

Nothing much happened in the next few days. Thursday, Harry and Rob took a detour on the way home to check out Wilton Water. The level was down a bit, but the main change was that the footpath round the reservoir had been sealed off at both ends by high mesh fences.

'Bummer!' growled Rob, hooking his fingers through the mesh and shaking it. 'I was dying to see what's left of Hopwood Mill. Now we can't get near.'

Harry shook his head. 'I don't know why old Well 'ard bothered sending that note round, it's like a flippin' prison camp. Only needs towers with lights and machine guns.'

Rob pulled a face. 'Probably putting them up tomorrow.' He hacked at the turf with the toe of his shoe. 'We could tunnel under though – the mesh doesn't continue underground.'

Harry tried a bit of hacking himself. He grinned. 'Sound idea, my friend. Got to get in somehow – I promised my sister an adventure.' He gazed through the fence at the darkening water. '*The Phantom of Wilton Water,* starring Harry and Bethan Midgley. Best supporting actor, Rob Hattersley.'

'Clown.' Rob turned to leave, and groaned. 'Oh no.'

Carl Hopwood was leaning in the gateway with his hands in his pockets, watching them. He smiled unpleasantly. 'What do you scruffs think you're doing? Didn't you get the Head's note?'

'We're just looking,' growled Rob.

'Yeah,' sneered Hopwood, 'and I'm just looking at *you.*' He nodded towards the fence. 'My dad had that put up. He didn't go to all that trouble just so losers like you could do criminal damage to it.' He eyeballed them. 'We're a long way from school. Old Woollard might not be able to keep an eye on Wilton Water but we can, and we will. Me, Shaun and Nigel. We catch you here, we'll shove you into that mesh so hard you'll come out the other side as chips.'

The pair watched the bully depart. 'No wonder they haven't bothered with lights and machine guns,' muttered Harry.

TWENTY-FIVE

After tea, Harry pulled Bethan into his room, closed the door and asked, 'Have you been past the res lately?'

Bethan shook her head. 'Saturday was the last time, when I took the snapshot. Why?'

'It's fenced off, you can't get on the footpath.'

Bethan frowned. 'Who's done that? Why would they want to . . . ?'

'Carl reckons his stupid dad got it done, for safety. And Carl's made himself chief of the reservoir police. He caught me and Rob there just now.'

'What the heck's it got to do with *him,* the red-faced creep?'

Harry shrugged. 'You know what he's like, just because his dad's a councillor. Probably thinks nobody should get a look at the old mill 'cause it used to be theirs.'

Bethan looked at her brother. 'So what are you saying, Harry – that we should just forget about our investigation? Our first genuine adventure?'

Harry shook his head. 'I'm not saying that at all.' He grinned. 'Think about it, Sis. It'll be a *bigger* adventure, won't it, high steel fences and Carl's performing cave trolls to watch out for. We'll have to be ice cool, totally focused.'

Bethan smiled. 'So we go for it?'

Harry nodded. 'When d'you want to start?'

'Well . . .' His sister thought for a moment. 'I think we ought to wait till after the Hallowe'en Hop. I haven't made my costume yet, and I won't be able to focus on anything else till it's done.'

'That's eight days,' said Harry. 'With a bit of luck, they'll have got the water level right down and there'll be something to see. What're you going as, by the way?'

Bethan shrugged. 'I'm thinking of going as a

witch's familiar. A black cat. It's a dead simple costume to make – black leotard, tail, mask with ears and whiskers, maybe a broomstick to ride on. It doesn't matter really – Aly's bound to win as the ghost. Hey.' She smiled. 'Maybe the ghost's guarding a treasure chest. We could end up millionaires.'

TWENTY-SIX

Friday evening, Hopwood House. The family at dinner: Councillor Reginald Hopwood, his wife Felicity and their son, Carl. The dining room is large, the table long. At one time, staff cooked and served all meals eaten here, but this enviable way of life began to fade when the waters closed over Hopwood Mill, and died altogether in Reginald's grandfather's time. Now, meals are Felicity's job. Today she's cooked pasta, and the portraits of old Josiah and his wife scowl down in disapproval at the food and the domestic arrangement generally.

Carl sliced open a sachet of ravioli, watched

the mince ooze out. *One day*, he promised him-self, *I'll do that to Harry Midgley.*

'Carl?'

'Y–yes, Dad?' Reginald bullied his son, which encouraged Carl to bully others.

'You *are* keeping a lookout at the reservoir, as I asked?'

Carl nodded. 'Yes, Dad. I scared two scruffs off yesterday, and today there was nobody.' He looked smug. 'They might not take much notice of old Woollard, but they don't mess with *me.*'

His father nodded. 'Good lad.'

Felicity frowned. 'I don't understand your interest in keeping people away from the reservoir, Reggie.' She resented his using Carl as a watchman.

Reginald bullied his wife as well as his son. 'There are lots of things *you* don't understand, Fliss,' he grated. 'Things about *my* family, *my* village. You're not *required* to understand them, and neither is Carl. *I'm* the councillor – *I'll* do the understanding. Your role is to support me by doing exactly as I say.'

'Yes, Reggie,' murmured Felicity. She knew

she ought to assert herself, but it never seemed quite the right time.

The time was at hand, though she didn't know it.

TWENTY-SEVEN

'Now then, Councillor.' Stan Fox greeted Reginald Hopwood as he plonked two tankards on the table. The councillor nodded and sat down. It was Saturday lunch time. The Feathers was busy. 'You wanted to see me?' said Fox.

Hopwood nodded. 'I'm a bit concerned about the reservoir job, Fox. Public safety.'

'*Safety?*' The reporter looked surprised. 'When I walked past this morning the place was like a fortress. Steel fencing, big red notices. I think Forgan's got safety pretty well covered.'

'Yes, but all the same.' Hopwood took a pull at

85

his pint, set down the tankard. 'A piece in the paper wouldn't do any harm. You know – heavy machinery, treacherous mud. That sort of thing.'

Fox grinned. 'Not to mention ghosts.'

Hopwood glanced up sharply. '*Ghosts?*'

The reporter nodded. 'Some chap rang the newsroom Sunday morning, reckoned his daughter's friend had captured the ghost of Wilton Water on camera. Wanted a reporter round to have a look.'

'Did you send someone?'

'No, it was Sunday, only one man in. I might have sent a junior round Monday but the same guy rang back, said it was a mistake.'

'Ah.' The councillor relaxed. 'Where'd he live, this chap?'

'Oh – Trough Lane, I think.' He nodded. 'Yes, Trough Lane. Name of Crabtree.'

Hopwood grunted. 'Nutter, by the sound of it.'

Fox nodded. 'Maybe. I like to keep an open mind.'

'Yes, but . . .' The councillor frowned. 'I shudder to think what'd happen if you *ran* a story like that, Fox. Take more than steel fencing to keep folk out then.'

'Yes well, it isn't going to happen.' The reporter lifted his tankard. 'Drink up, Councillor, it's my shout.'

TWENTY-EIGHT

Thursday, half past twelve. The gaunt young man stepped into the councillor's path as he was making his way towards the pub, offered a magazine. 'Here y'are, sir – *Big Issue*, top quality at a bargain price.'

Reginald Hopwood was in an unusually foul mood, even for him. Tomorrow, Wilton Primary School was holding its Hallowe'en Hop, and as Chair of Governors he'd agreed to judge the fancy-dress competition. *Hallowe'en Hop*, snarled a furious voice inside his head. *More like Hallowe'en flop*. He didn't like kids, despised teachers and detested fancy-dress competitions.

Aged nine he'd gone in for one, done up as a carrot. He hadn't wanted to – felt totally daft with those long green feathers sprouting out of the top of his head, but his mother had made the costume herself and was proud of it. The kids laughed and shoved him about, just as he knew they would, and of course he didn't win. It had taken him weeks afterwards to corner his tormentors one by one and beat them up.

'Buy a *Big Issue*, sir – help the homeless.'

With the vendor directly in front of him, the councillor had no choice but to stop. '*You* again,' he spat. 'I told you before – get a proper job and stop harassing innocent pedestrians. You're a disgrace to the village, the country and yourself.'

'I *had* a job, sir. A good one. Then they made me redundant and I couldn't find anything else. My wife left me, took the kids. I got depressed, couldn't go out, lost the house. It can happen to anyone, sir – it could happen to *you*.'

Hopwood scoffed. 'You obviously don't know who I am, you cheeky young beggar. I'm Councillor Hopwood. My family practically built this village, so you'd better get out of my way or

I'll call the police.' He smiled twistedly. 'You'll be depressed *then* all right.'

The vendor stepped aside and called after Hopwood as he strode away. 'Everything changes, sir. Nothing stays the same, even for important men like you. Have a nice day.'

TWENTY-NINE

Christa smiled at the thin black cat. 'You look really cool, sweetheart.'

'Do I, Mum, honestly?' Bethan looked at her mother through translucent green eyes.

'Definitely. Original or not, if you don't win that competition there's no justice.'

Bethan grinned behind the furry mask. 'I'll get done by Aly if I do, after I made her change her outfit.'

Christa shook her head. 'It would have been wrong of Alison to go as my poor aunt, Bethan.'

'Great, great aunt,' corrected Harry.

'Doesn't matter,' snapped his mother, 'she

was my family. *Our* family. It's better this way.'

It was five to six. Christa picked up the car keys and moved to the door. Bethan picked up her tail and followed. Harry went up to his room.

Norah Crabtree tore her eyes away from the screen for a second as Alison crossed the room. 'D'you want a lift, lovey?'

'No, Mum, it's all right.'

'You sure?' Her mother had already returned to the six o'clock news. 'Bit chilly out, dressed skimpy like that.'

'It's OK.' Alison paused by the door. 'Do I look all right?'

'You look a picture, love,' said her father, gazing at the newsreader. 'Don't talk to strangers, don't get in anyone's car. Shut the door on your way out. I'll collect you at nine o'clock.'

Alison threw a hoodie round her shoulders and set off along Trough Lane. The hem of the old black dress scraped the ground as she walked, and the wind blew cold round her white bony ankles.

* * *

Reginald paused in the hallway, called up the stairs. 'Right, I'm off then.'

'Yes, well.' Felicity's voice floated faintly from above. 'Drive carefully, have a lovely time.'

'Lovely time,' snarled the councillor, not loudly enough to be heard upstairs. 'Fat chance of that. Two hours perched on a hard, child-size chair, watching a mob of future asbos cavorting in tatty, home-made costumes to hideous garage music, whatever that is.' He shrugged into a bulky sheepskin car coat, opened the door. 'Being expected to eat ghastly toad-shaped cakes made by some sanitarily-challenged mother in God knows what sort of kitchen, washed down with some fizzy red stuff labelled blood.'

The Chair of Governors drove off, still chuntering to himself.

THIRTY

Eight o'clock. At Wilton Primary, the Hallowe'en Hop was in full swing. The children were having the terrific time they'd anticipated, and their Chair of Governors was every bit as miserable as he'd expected to be.

The music was loud, the lighting and decorations awesome, the food gruesome and plentiful. Best of all, there were some truly stunning costumes. Witches and wizards cavorted under spotlights which struck flashes of metallic brilliance from their sequins. Bats, cats, spiders and toads capered among them, ugliness made beautiful by the multicoloured jewels of their eyes. Only one dancer was plain: a thin, white-faced figure all in black who swayed sinuously to a rhythm all her own: who caught Reginald Hopwood's eye precisely because of her gaunt, haunting plainness.

'Mr Hopwood?' The headteacher bent close to Reginald's ear. 'I wonder if you've spotted the costume you feel is the most original?' She smiled, watching the children. 'They certainly haven't made your task an easy one, have they?'

Hopwood forced a grin, shook his head. 'No, Miss Gadd, they haven't.' He'd just eaten something called a batburger, and its aftertaste was making him suspect it might have been made with an actual bat. 'However, I *have now* made my choice.'

'Splendid!' smiled Miss Gadd. 'We'll let them dance for five more minutes, then I'll stop the music and you can venture into the throng and lead the winner onto the platform.'

Reginald nodded. 'Fine.'

'And in the meantime, please feel free to enjoy another of the Sexton's batburgers.'

He didn't know why he felt drawn to the dancer in the long black dress. It wasn't an attractive costume, and the child had smeared far too much mascara round her eyes. She reminded him of some Goths he'd spotted once at Whitby, there for a Dracula bash. *She stands out,* he told himself. And she's original.

The music stopped, prompting groans of protest. Hopwood rose stiffly, scanning the restless crowd. The girl in black had disappeared.

THIRTY-ONE

As the music stopped, Alison slipped out to the cloakroom to put the finishing touch to her costume. She'd noticed the Chair of Governors watching her, and was pretty sure he meant to award her the prize. *Wait till you see this*, she thought, twisting a tap and holding her hand in the flow. *Come on water, warm up.*

Reginald Hopwood was standing in the middle of the hall, cutting his eyes this way and that, trying to hide his irritation. Alison wound her way through the crowd, leaving a splashy trail till she stood in front of him, drenched from head to toe. A puddle began to form under the hem of the bedraggled dress, mascara scored tear tracks down her cheeks. Children gasped and stared as she stood absolutely still, pointing a long pale finger at the floor.

'Wh . . . why are you wet?' croaked Hopwood.

Alison smiled. 'It's part of the costume, I'm the ghost of Wilton Water.'

'There *is* no—' The councillor seemed agitated. 'What's *that* to do with Hallowe'en?' He grabbed the girl's hand. 'What's your name, girl?'

'Alison, sir. Alison Crabtree. I wanted something spooky – original. Nobody's ever . . .'

'N . . . no,' stammered the Chair of Governors. 'I mean yes, it *is* original. Very.' He began tugging Alison towards the platform. 'You win, of course you do.' He half-dragged her across the floor amid a clatter of applause.

As Hopwood thrust the prize at Alison, a camera flashed. The photographer smiled. 'Hi, I'm Bill from the *Echo*. Can I get your name, sweetheart?'

'Yes, it's Alison Crabtree.'

'Good. And who've you come as, Alison?'

'The g . . . ghost of Wilton Water.' She was cold, her teeth were chattering.

'Has she a *name*, this ghost?'

'Well . . .' Flustered by the occasion and by Hopwood's odd behaviour, Alison blurted, 'Hettie Daynes, I suppose . . . she *might* have been Hettie Daynes when she . . .'

'No name,' snapped the Chair of Governors. 'Just call her the ghost.' He glared at the photographer. 'I'm Councillor Hopwood. Stanley Fox is a friend. If I read that name in the paper you're in big trouble, understand?'

The man shrugged. 'Sure. It's all the same to me, Councillor.' He pocketed the pad, hung his paraphernalia on a shoulder, nodded to the Head and strode away.

'Come, Alison, you silly girl,' said Miss Gadd. 'Let's get you into some dry clothes.' She smiled at Hopwood. 'Thank you *so* much, Councillor – I do hope you've enjoyed the evening.'

Hopwood managed to smile back. 'Very much, Headteacher.' *Like you'd enjoy having a bolt hammered through your kneecap*, he thought but didn't say.

Alison followed Miss Gadd to the staffroom.

THIRTY-TWO

Her mother smiled as Bethan slid into the passenger seat. 'Good time, sweetheart? Did you win?'

Bethan nodded her head, then shook it. 'Yes I had a good time, no I didn't win.' She smiled. 'Aly did.'

Christa nodded. 'That's what you hoped would happen, isn't it?'

'Ye-es.' Bethan looked sidelong at her mother. 'Didn't quite go the way *you* wanted though, Mum.'

'What d'you mean, love?' Christa started the engine, eased out of the parking space.

'Well, there was this guy from the *Echo*, Mum. Bill. He took Aly's picture, asked her name and who she'd come as.'

Christa nodded, steering the car through the gateway. 'Right.'

'Yes, but when she said the ghost of Wilton Water, Bill asked if the ghost had a name.' Bethan pulled a face. 'I guess it took Aly by surprise, because she said it might be Hettie Daynes.'

'Ah.' Christa hung a left, accelerated. 'Exactly what I'd hoped to avoid. Now my poor aunt's name'll be plastered all over the *Echo*, and every superstitious so-and-so for miles round will believe she haunts the reservoir.'

Bethan shook her head. 'I'm sorry, Mum, but Aly didn't do it on purpose. She was wet and freezing, and the question took her by surprise. You're not *too* mad at her, are you?'

Christa sighed. 'I don't suppose so, love. She didn't mean to break her promise – she's a scatterbrain I expect, like her mother.'

'And anyway it won't be in the paper.'

'What d'you mean – *why* won't it?'

Bethan shook her head. 'Councillor Hopwood was really weird about it – told Bill he'd get him done if he put the name in the *Echo*. He's to call her the ghost.'

'Really? *Well*.' Christa chuckled. 'I never thought I'd have reason to be grateful to that pompous windbag.'

THIRTY-THREE

I *hope you've enjoyed the evening.* Reginald Hopwood slammed home the gearshift and stamped on the pedal. The classic Rover roared down the schoolyard and swung into the road on screeching tyres. *I should've quoted Groucho Marx – I've had a wonderful evening, but this wasn't it.*

He scowled through the windscreen. *That girl, Alison Crabtree. Where have I heard her name lately – Crabtree?*

It came to him as he negotiated a sharp bend, taking it wide. *Fox of course, Saturday. Crabtree was the guy who phoned the Echo, said he'd got a snapshot of the ghost. Called back later to say it was all a mistake. I bet Alison's the guy's daughter. I bet that's where she got the idea for her costume.*

Can't actually be a snapshot though, can there? Nobody's ever photographed a ghost – not even the so-called psychic investigators. Because there's no such thing as a ghost, that's why. It's gross superstition, like vampires and werewolves.

Hopwood sighed, sat back in the soft leather seat, told himself to relax. *Of course* there was no snapshot – the guy'd said so himself, hadn't he? All a mistake.

Yes, murmured the voice inside his head. *But what about Stan Fox? He'll see the kid's name in the paper, spot the coincidence: guy rings up about the ghost, then a kid of the same name comes dressed as the ghost. That damn photographer tells Fox what I said about not mentioning Hettie Daynes in print, and he connects it with me being paranoid about keeping people away from the reservoir.*

He sighed again, shook his head. *All I can do is keep my head down and hope he won't follow it up.*

The Rover sped through the dark, squashing small furry things all the way.

THIRTY-FOUR

Curiosity was Stan Fox's nickname. Curiosity Fox they called him at the *Echo*, because he loved sticking his nose into things. Sniffing around. Hoping to flush out something interesting. Stan's curiosity was what made him a good journalist.

The morning after Hallowe'en, Stan's curiosity was stirred by a coincidence. Stan Fox didn't believe in coincidence. He believed that when two things come together to form what people call a coincidence, there's always a reason. It's often a hidden reason, needing a sharp nose like Stan's to sniff it out.

It was Bill Rowntree's piece about the Hallowe'en Hop at Wilton Primary. The *Echo* published on Thursdays, and next Thursday's edition would carry a full page of pics and captions about the various Hallowe'en events in the area. The dummy of this page was displayed on Fox's screen, and he was reading the caption under Rowntree's photo.

Ten-year-old Alison Crabtree, it read, *winner of Wilton Primary School's most original Hallowe'en costume competition. Alison came as the ghost which some local people claim to have seen at Wilton Water. The competition was judged by Councillor Reginald Hopwood, the school's Chair of Governors.*

Fox frowned. *Crabtree. Now where . . . ah, yes.* His features cleared. *The guy who claimed to have a snapshot of the ghost. His name was Crabtree. I wonder . . .*

He walked over to Rowntree's desk. 'That kid, Bill – the competition winner at Wilton Prim. We'll have her home address, won't we?'

Bill Rowntree nodded. 'Sure – we put a glossy print in the post for kids. Hang on.' His fingers pecked at his keyboard. 'Here y'are – ten Trough Lane, Wilton.'

Fox nodded. 'As I thought.'

'What is it, Stan?'

Fox shrugged. 'Guy phoned from that address a few days back. Claimed to have a snapshot of the ghost.' He grinned. 'Probably his daughter in her Hallowe'en get-up.'

Rowntree nodded. 'Probably.' He looked at Fox. 'Funny do with your mate the councillor, by the way.'

'How d'you mean?'

'Well, I asked the kid if the ghost had a name. She said it might be Hettie Daynes, and Hopwood told me not to print it. Threatened to drop me in it with you if I did.' He pulled a face. 'So I haven't. Weird, though.'

'Hmmm.' Fox squeezed the man's shoulder. 'Don't worry about it, Bill. Bit strange, old Hopwood. Always was.'

He returned to his own desk and sat, gazing at something only he could see.

THIRTY-FIVE

W ednesday lunch time. Harry and Rob on
the school playing field. A chill, misty day
with winter on its breath. 'How's this for an idea?'
asked Harry.

Rob, shoulders hunched, hands in pockets,
looked at his friend. 'What?'

'It's Bonfire Night, right?'

'Not much gets past you, sucker. What of it?'

'Well, we need to get a look at the reservoir
now the water's low. Carl and the cave trolls won't
be there tonight.'

Rob pulled a face. 'Won't they?'

''Course not. Carl'll be at the bonfire – his

dad's the boss of it. And where Carl is, there're the cave trolls.' Harry grinned. 'We'll have a clear field, old mate, plus our folks'll think we're at the bonfire.'

'It'll be flipping dark,' grumbled Rob.

Harry nodded. 'Obviously. I don't mean we go wading knee-deep in mud. I just want to check out the old mill. You in or not?'

'In, I suppose,' growled Rob. 'We can catch the bonfire after.'

As her brother and his friend strolled round the playing field at the big kids' school in Rawton, Bethan and Alison were doing the same at Wilton Primary. It must be true that great minds think alike, because Bethan was talking about the reservoir too.

'I'll tell my mum I'm off to the fire,' she said. 'She comes as well, but not till later.' She smiled. 'She'll tell Harry to keep an eye on me, but I bet *he*'ll want to check out the res. What d'you think?'

'Hmmm?' Alison was wired to the Walkman she'd won at the Hallowe'en Hop. Bethan scowled. 'Turn that thing off for a minute, Aly,

109

and listen.' She went through the whole thing again. 'So, what d'you think?'

Alison shrugged. 'I'll come.' She pulled a face. 'Don't know why you want to go scaring yourself though. And I'll only go if Harry does.'

THIRTY-SIX

The Midgleys' kitchen, six o'clock. Christa looked at Harry. 'I'm trusting you to keep an eye on your sister, Harry. I'll be along around eight. Till then I want you to keep Bethan well back from the fire, and away from the numpties who throw bangers. Is that understood?'

Harry nodded. 'I promise she'll be well away from the fire, and no bangers'll come anywhere near us.' He'd talked with Bethan earlier. They weren't going straight to the bonfire, so his promise was an easy one to make. All he had to do was make sure they were there by the time their mother arrived.

Bethan giggled as they hurried along under the streetlamps. 'You're a lying toad, Bro. *She'll be well away from the fire.* Lie for England, you could.'

'I didn't lie,' protested Harry. 'You *will* be well away – quarter of a mile away.'

'Yeah, right.'

Rob joined them at the end of the road, and Alison was waiting by the reservoir gateway. It was cold. The four were bundled up in scarves, jeans and hoodies.

Harry looked at Alison. 'Any sign of life, Aly?'

Alison shook her head. 'Not if you mean Carl.' She shrugged. 'Nobody's gonna come with the footpath closed, not even dog-walkers.'

Harry nodded. 'Come on then, we haven't got all night.'

They approached the fence. Bethan hooked her fingers through the mesh, pressed her nose to it. 'How do we get through *this*?'

'We don't,' said Rob. 'We go round it.'

'*Round* it?' Harry looked at him. 'I thought we'd decided to tunnel under.'

Rob shook his head. 'If we do that, some-body'll notice. They'll fill it in, and we'll have to scrape it out afresh every time we come. No.' He turned and pointed. 'The fence went to the water's edge, but the water's gone right down. If we slide down the bank, we can walk on the mud till we're past the fence. It's only a few strides.'

'*Muddy* strides,' said Harry. 'We should've come in wellies.'

'Don't be such a wimp,' mocked Rob. 'What's a bit of mud?'

'A big deal if you're *our* mum,' sighed Bethan. She grinned. 'I vote we go for it though.'

They sat on their bottoms in the wet grass and lowered themselves till their shoes sank into soft mud. Rob led the way as they squelched through the ooze. Mud sucks, strides weren't possible. They found they were pulling their feet free at every pace. Alison lost a shoe and had to plunge her hand into the mire to get it back. 'Pooh!' she gasped. 'It pongs a bit, this stuff.'

As they pressed on, a glow appeared in the sky to their right. 'There goes the bonfire,' murmured Harry. 'His majesty Councillor Hopwood has ignited the conflagration.'

'I hope he's dumped his swamp-thing son on top as a guy,' growled Rob.

Bethan looked down at her mud-plastered jeans. 'It's *us* who're the swamp-things,' she laughed.

The fence behind them, they turned shoreward and scrambled up the banking. Rockets were sowing stars in the sky, and flashes were followed by bangs. As they stood, stamping their feet to loosen clods of mud, something moved in the dark between the trees. Bethan saw it first. 'What the heck's *that*?' she croaked.

'*What?*' cried Rob. '*Where?*' They were glancing wildly about them when a man's voice called out, 'Who's there: what the *heck* do you kids think you're playing at?'

They froze.

THIRTY-SEVEN

The dry pallets at the base of the stack had got the bonfire off to a brisk start. Reginald Hopwood stepped back. Three volunteer stewards had spaced themselves at intervals round the stack. They were burly villagers, whose main job was to prevent anybody getting too close to the blaze, but they'd move swiftly to curb any outbreak of hooliganism.

Hopwood scanned the gathering till he located his son. Carl was taking snapshots of the fire with his mobi, watched by Nigel Stocks and Shaun Modley. The councillor stared at them till

115

Carl looked across, then beckoned him. The sidekicks came too.

'I need you to check out the reservoir,' he told the trio.

'Oh, Da–ad,' protested Carl. 'Not tonight. We'll miss the fireworks, and besides nobody'll bother with the res on Bonfire Night. They're all *here*.'

His father looked at him. '*Are* they? Can you be sure about that?'

'Well no, but . . .'

'There you are then.'

Carl looked surly. 'What *is* it about the res anyway, Dad? Why should *you* care if plonkers put themselves in danger? It isn't fair, me and the lads were looking forward to watching the fireworks.'

The councillor's features reddened. 'The *lads* can please themselves,' he spluttered. 'They don't live under my roof, eat my food. You *do*. Which means you do *exactly* as I tell you at all times. Is that clear?'

'Y–yes, Dad.' Carl hated looking a prat in front of his friends, but he'd always been scared of his father. He looked at Shaun and Nigel. 'Coming?'

Shaun shuffled his feet, looked at the ground.

'No, I reckon I'll stick around, mate, if that's all right.'

Nigel nodded. 'Yeah, me too. We'll see you later, eh?'

'Thanks a bunch,' snarled Carl. 'Good to have mates you can count on.' He turned his back on the fire, slunk away. It'd be woe betide any kid he found near Wilton Water tonight.

THIRTY-EIGHT

'Wh . . . who is it?' Bethan moved closer to her brother.

'Dunno, Sis. Get ready to run.'

Rob snorted. 'In *that* mud? No chance.'

'It's a man with glasses,' whispered Alison.

Harry glanced at her. 'Glasses – you *sure*?' There was comfort in glasses; ghosts and monsters don't wear them.

Alison nodded. 'Look.'

The man came out of the trees. Fireglow reflected in the round lenses of his spectacles.

Rob laughed with relief. 'It's Steve,' he said. 'Steve Wood.' He called out. 'It's OK, Mister

Wood, it's only us. We talked here a while back.'

The historian approached. He wasn't smiling. 'I know,' he growled, 'but that was tea time. You kids shouldn't be here this late – what if I'd been a serial killer or something? What're you doing, anyway?'

'We came to check out the mill,' said Harry. 'The one you told us about.'

Wood nodded. 'Hopwood Mill. It's just along there, but it's too dark to see much, and it's highly dangerous to walk on that reservoir bed as you've just done. It drops off steeply into deep water.'

'OK,' said Rob. 'We get the message, but we might as well have a quick look now we're here.'

The historian sighed. 'It's easier to get in and out at the other end. I'll show you. We pass the mill on the way.'

They followed Steve along the footpath. Flashes lit the sky.

Steve stopped, pointed. 'There, see?'

They peered across the mud, saw lengths of crumbled wall, none more than a metre high.

'Is that *it*?' asked Harry. 'No chimney, no roofs?'

Wood chuckled. 'They didn't leave the chimney up, lad, they re-used the stone. Took the roofs off as well. Yorkshire stone, expensive. It's in the village, I'll show you sometime. Come on.'

'Can't we just go down for a minute?' asked Bethan.

Steve shook his head. 'No way, young lady. I told you, it's dangerous. Come back in daylight if you can dodge the workmen, but don't come by yourself. And *don't* tell anybody I suggested it or you'll get me shot.'

At the west end of the reservoir was the dam wall, the overflow, the diggers and the dumpsters. This was where the work went on by day. There was a fence across the footpath, but this one was movable because the workmen had to come and go. Steve Wood lifted the tubular steel pole and bent one end of the fencing inward to make a narrow gap between it and the boundary wall. He ushered them through and swung the pole back into position.

'Right,' he said, sternly. 'Off to the bonfire now, and remember what I said. No more night expeditions, OK?'

Rob nodded for all of them. 'OK, Mister Wood.

Daylight only, and *you* never said we could.'
He grinned. 'In fact we've never heard of you.'

Steve smiled and nodded. 'That's about right, lad. G'night.'

THIRTY-NINE

Carl kicked a pebble off the bank, watched it plop in the mud. He had on his brand new Nikes. *There's no way I'm wading through that in these.*

Trouble was, there were footprints. Loads of them. They showed up every time a firework exploded. It looked like a bunch of people had squelched through the goo. He could go back to the fire and report all quiet. He might even catch the fireworks, but tomorrow was Thursday. Thursdays, his dad had lunch at The Feathers. What if he took it into his head to check out the res? He was daft enough. He'd see the prints.

He'd know Carl must've seen them too. Life at home would be even more dodgy than usual.

Muttering to himself, he sat down and unlaced his trainers. He'd roll up his jeans and go barefoot with the Nikes round his neck. 'And I wouldn't be you whoever you are, when I catch up with you,' he hissed.

Rocket flashes showed Carl that nobody was in front of him. He rounded the fence, scrambled up the bank and tried wiping his feet on grass. This didn't work. His socks would be plastered with stinky gloop. *Not my fault*, he thought. *Dad's fault for being a screwed-up nutcase.*

With the Nikes back on, he started along the footpath.

He was pretty sure the intruders were long gone by now, and that was fine – he didn't fancy tackling a bunch of kids without backup. But he wasn't going to let his dad accuse him of not doing a thorough job. *I tracked 'em*, he'd say, *made sure they'd left.*

They hadn't though, had they? He stopped, screwed up his eyes. *Somebody's out there, by the mill, and he's by himself.* He smiled. *Boy, is he going to pay for the hassle he's put me through.*

At that moment, a brilliant flash lit the sky and Carl saw his intended target clearly. She was standing two metres above the mud, on nothing more solid than air.

FORTY

'Well *that* was a big waste of time,' grumbled Harry, staring moodily at the bonfire.

'Yes it was,' agreed his sister, examining her shoes in the firelight. 'And look at the state of these trainers. Mum'll go mad.'

'Don't be such miseries,' said Alison. 'We're here before your mum, *and* we haven't missed the fireworks. That's what matters.'

''S all right for *you*,' snarled Bethan. 'Your mum won't even look at your shoes, and if she does she won't give a stuff. You're lucky.'

'We're *all* lucky,' put in Rob. 'Carl's not here.'

Harry's eyes searched the crowd. 'No he isn't,

is he? His dad is, and both cave trolls, but not his great pink self.'

'Probably drowning some kittens,' growled Rob, 'or torturing a robin. You know how he likes a laugh.'

'Ah, *there* you are!' Christa approached, smiling. 'Am I in time for the fireworks?'

Bethan nodded. 'Yes, Mum, Councillor Hopwood's getting the stewards together, they're about to start.'

It was a brilliant display, same as every year. The village traders clubbed together to buy the fireworks and no expense was spared. It was the one occasion when all the people of Wilton came together, and it was safer than having kids messing with fireworks of their own.

The show had reached its usual climax – salvo after salvo of large costly rockets whooshing into the sky trailing clouds of glory, when Harry spotted Carl Hopwood. He was walking through the crowd like a zombie, staring straight ahead as if nothing at all was happening above. As Harry watched, the lad approached his father, tugged at his sleeve to get his attention and spoke, gesturing back the way he'd come. To Harry's horror, the councillor shook his son off and fetched him a terrific clout across the side of the head, knocking him to the ground.

FORTY-ONE

'What's happened?' asked Christa, glancing to where a knot of men stood looking at something on the ground. The last shoal of stars had blinked out, leaving their green phantoms in front of her eyes. 'Has somebody been hurt?'

Harry nodded. 'Yes, but not by a firework.'

'What, then? I was watching the rockets.'

'Everybody was. I bet I'm the only one who saw.'

'Saw *what*, love?'

'The councillor hit Carl, really hard. He fell down, they're all gawping at him.'

As he spoke Carl sat up, one hand pressed to

his cheek. The men stepped back. Councillor Hopwood bent, gripped his son's elbow and pulled him to his feet. The boy looked groggy but his father ushered him away at once, through the circle of spectators, heading for the Rover.

'What a brute,' gasped Christa. 'He's lucky everybody was busy watching the sky. I expect he'll claim the boy fainted or something.'

'Yeah,' said Harry. 'Pity that photographer wasn't here.'

What's he called, Aly?'

'Bill.'

'That's the one. Shame Bill wasn't here with his camera.' He smiled tightly. 'Likes his picture in the *Echo*, our Councillor, but I bet he wouldn't want an action shot of himself damn near knocking his son's head off.'

'Front page,' grinned Rob. '*Councillor Reginald Hopwood enjoys an intimate moment with his son during Wilton's annual bonfire celebration. Minutes after this picture was taken, Carl was rushed to Rawton General Hospital where his head was sewn back on.*'

'Idiot,' growled Harry.

'Not something to joke about really, boys,'

murmured Christa. 'Makes you wonder what goes on behind the curtains up at Hopwood House.'

'*Hopwood's House of Horrors,*' intoned the incorrigible Rob. '*Featuring Raving Reginald, Rawton's Rotten Ratbag.*'

FORTY-TWO

Felicity Hopwood was at the window when the Rover pulled up in front of the garage. She'd been watching the rockets and Roman candles over the village rooftops. Felicity enjoyed fireworks, but never accompanied her husband anywhere unless it was absolutely necessary.

Reginald had stopped the car to let Carl out. As soon as she saw her son, Felicity knew something had happened. Carl didn't look like a boy coming home from an exciting event. There was something hangdog about the way he waited for his father to put the car away. It was a look his mother had seen many times before. As the pair approached the house, Felicity stepped back and let the curtain fall.

Carl entered the room first. Felicity greeted him with the bright smile she wore when she didn't feel like smiling. 'Hello, Carl – nice time?' The bruised cheek and swollen ear made his face look lopsided.

He shook his head and mumbled, 'Does it *look* like I had a nice time? I saw this woman. She was a ghost but Dad says—'

Reginald loomed scowling in the doorway. 'Dad says get yourself off to bed, *now*.' Carl shot his mother a scornful look, then turned and slunk out. As he passed his father, Reginald raised a hand as if to hit him. The boy flinched, and Reginald laughed contemptuously. Felicity looked at her husband with loathing.

'You hit him. A little boy. I don't know how you can live with yourself.'

Reginald laughed again. 'Certainly I hit him. He deserved it, showing me up in front of my friends.'

'You show *yourself* up,' murmured his wife, 'and you don't deserve to *have* friends.' She was trembling. 'D'you know what *I* wonder, Reginald?

132

I wonder how you'd fare if you were ever foolish enough to strike somebody your own size.'

'Ha!' Her husband glared. 'There *is* nobody my size,' he snarled. 'Not in Wilton, nor in Rawton. You married the cock of the heap, Felicity – not that you appreciate it or anything like that. Where's my supper?'

Felicity locked eyes with him. 'Your supper's wherever you find it, you contemptible bully. I hope it chokes you.'

FORTY-THREE

'Whoa!' cried Christa, as she followed Harry and Bethan into the porch. 'Don't you *dare* track those trainers across my kitchen floor.' She gave them a suspicious look. 'How've they got into that state anyway – there was hardly any mud on the Green.'

Harry pulled a face. 'We . . . called at the res on our way, Mum. My idea, sorry.'

His mother sighed. 'If you were sorry, Harry, you wouldn't have done it. Your father was forever saying he was sorry, but it didn't stop him doing the same thing over and over.'

Harry shook his head. 'I'm *nothing* like

Dad – it does my head in when you say that.'

'I'm sorry, love. Of *course* you're not like him. It's just that I've asked you not to take Bethan near the reservoir, especially in the dark, and you did so regardless.'

'It's not *all* Harry's fault,' put in Bethan. 'I'm interested in the old mill too, and—' She nearly mentioned the ghost, but stopped herself in time. 'And I nag him to take me.'

'Yes well,' said Christa, 'we'll say no more about it, at least not tonight.' She smiled. 'Decide who's having the first shower, and I'll put the kettle on for hot chocolate.'

Brother and sister slept like logs that night, but their mother did not. She lay thinking about Wilton Water, Hettie Daynes and the strange behaviour of Councillor Hopwood. On the face of it, the three topics were unconnected.

But *were* they?

FORTY-FOUR

Carl was sitting on the bed, hands clamped between his knees, staring at the rug. He looked up as his mother came into the room. She saw that he'd been crying, sat down and put an arm round him. 'Where was the woman you saw? What makes you think she was a ghost?'

Carl shook off the arm, turned his face away. 'On the reservoir, standing in the air.'

'What d'you mean, *in the air*? Was she *flying*?'

He shook his head. 'No, of *course* she wasn't flying, you daft beggar. She was *standing*. Six feet above the mud.'

He was shivering. She reached for him but he

batted her hand away. 'Why were you at the reservoir, Carl? You were meant to be at the fire.'

'Dad sent me to see if any kids were there.'

'*Why?*' Felicity sighed in exasperation. 'I don't understand. Do *you* know why he's the way he is about Wilton Water?'

Carl shrugged. 'Safety, he reckons. Barmy if you ask me.'

'No.' His mother shook her head. 'Your father isn't barmy, Carl, but something's worrying him.' She touched the boy's cheek with her fingertips. 'So you told him what you'd seen, and then he hit you?'

Carl jerked his head back. 'Yes. Some of his friends were there. He called me a blithering idiot, showing him up. Then he knocked me down.'

'And none of these friends protested. About his hitting you, I mean?'

'I don't know, do I? I was stunned. Maybe they didn't see, everybody was watching the rockets. And anyway you've no room to talk. *You* never protest.'

'I do the best I can,' murmured Felicity. 'It isn't easy for me either, you know.' She touched her son's hair. 'As for what you saw at the reservoir, try to put it out of your mind. It was dark, there were lights in the sky. Smoke. You certainly saw *something*, but perhaps it wasn't quite what it appeared to be.' She stood up, pecked his swollen cheek. 'Sleep well, darling.'

FORTY-FIVE

The *Rawton Echo* came out every Thursday. The day after Bonfire Night, certain people could hardly wait to see a copy of the paper. Most impatient was Councillor Hopwood. He bought an early edition on his way to The Feathers and paged through it as he walked along the street. He found Bill's photo of Alison Crabtree in her wet costume and scanned the caption underneath.

Ten-year-old Alison Crabtree, winner of Wilton Primary School's most original Hallowe'en costume competition. Alison came as the ghost which some local people claim to have seen at Wilton

Water. The competition was judged by Councillor Reginald Hopwood, the school's Chair of Governors.

Reginald smiled, folded the paper and thrust it into his jacket pocket. The photographer had heeded his threat. The ghost was just a ghost. No name, which was good. His own name appeared though, and that was even better. He was so pleased, he forgot to swear at the *Big Issue* vendor who occupied his usual pitch.

The Crabtrees wanted to see the *Echo* too, but they had to wait till tea time. It was on the table, along with a stack of unironed washing and the cat when Alison got in from school. Her mother nodded towards it. 'It's open at the page, love. You look sensational.'

Alison gazed at the photo. She *did* look sensational. She also looked remarkably like the apparition Bethan had snapped at the res. The white make-up, pointing finger and bedraggled dress were absolutely spot-on. 'That is *so* cool,' she breathed.

'I'm cutting it out,' said her mother, 'when everybody's had a look. 'Tisn't every day someone in our family gets her picture in the paper.'

Alison smiled, shook her head. 'There's no need, Mum. They send a glossy in a few days. That'll be better.'

'It won't have the words underneath though,' said Norah. 'We'll keep both, and our Tony can scan it for your Auntie Shelley. She's out of it all, down there in Milton Keynes.'

FORTY-SIX

Not everybody was happy with Bill's snapshot. Carl Hopwood, who'd been kept at
home because of his bruised face, saw it in
the paper his father had left on the coffee table.
He gazed at it. *Try to put it out of your mind*,
his mother had said last night, and he *had* tried.
This stark reminder made him moan, so that
his mother looked up from her magazine.

'What is it, Carl?' She hadn't quite forgiven him
for calling her a daft beggar.

'This kid in the paper, Mum, look.' He held up
the *Echo*.

'Yes, your father showed it to me.'

'She's just like the woman I saw at the res. The ghost. It says local people have seen it, so why won't you and Dad believe *I* saw it?'

Felicity shook her head. 'It's a *story*, Carl. A local legend. Lots of places are said to have ghosts, and some people think they see them because they *expect* to. You know the story of the ghost of Wilton Water, so when you were alone in the dark by the reservoir, you *saw* her.'

'You mean I only *thought* I saw her?' He shook his head. 'She was *there* – I saw her like I see you now.'

His mother nodded. 'You saw her, Carl, but she came from your mind, not from the water. A psychologist would say she arose out of the cortex. These things happen, it doesn't mean people are lying.' She frowned. 'And it *certainly* doesn't justify knocking them about.'

Carl folded the paper, dropped it on the table. 'I don't want to be going there all the time, Mum. Will you talk to Dad?'

His mother nodded. 'I'll talk to him, certainly, but you know what he's like. We must hope this work on the reservoir will be finished soon, then perhaps your father will stop fussing.'

Carl shook his head. 'No, Mum, he won't. You know he won't. He'll just find something else to go on about.'

FORTY-SEVEN

'Mr Crabtree?' asked the man on the step. Tony shook his head. 'I'm Tony Crabtree, you probably want my dad.'

The man nodded. 'I'm seeking the gentleman who called the *Echo* recently about an unusual snapshot.' He smiled, stuck out a hand. 'I'm Stan Fox, Chief Reporter on the paper.'

'Oh.' Tony hesitated, then took the hand and shook it. 'Yes, that was my dad but he's out. So's my mum. They go to the supermarket Friday afternoons. I . . . didn't my dad call back to say it was all a mistake?'

Fox nodded. 'Yes, Tony, he did, but then one of

our photographers took this picture at the primary school last Friday.' He pulled a brown envelope from his coat pocket, slid out a glossy photograph and showed it to the youth. 'Is this young woman your sister?'

Tony nodded. 'Yes, that's our Alison. She won a fancy-dress competition. The pic was in yesterday's paper.' He frowned. 'What's this about, Mr Fox?'

Stan looked at him. 'Alison told our man she'd come as the ghost of Wilton Water. Your dad claimed he had a snapshot of that ghost. I was wondering . . .'

Tony shook his head. 'It wasn't a snap of our Alison, if *that's* what you were wondering.'

Fox pounced. '*What* wasn't?'

'The . . .' Realizing his mistake, Tony stammered, 'I . . . I mean we didn't take a picture of my sister in her costume, up the res. It wasn't a trick.'

Fox eyed him narrowly. 'So what *was* it, Tony?'

'A mistake, like my dad said. Look – I've got to go now, I'm shutting the door.'

He tried to shut it, but Fox stuck his shoe in

the way. 'Come on, lad, let me see what you've got.'

'I haven't got *anything*, Mr Fox.'

'Yes you have. They don't call me Curiosity Fox for nothing. I'm a dab-hand at sniffing out what's been did and what's been hid. All I'm asking is a quick peek. It's not for publication, I promise you.'

Tony hesitated, then gave in. 'Aw heck.' He opened the door, stepped aside. 'The thing is, Mr Fox, it's not our photo. Alison's friend took it, and she doesn't want owt in the *Echo* about it.'

The reporter smiled. 'Haven't I just promised not to publish, Tony? All I want's a quick shufti. Come on, there's a good lad.'

FORTY-EIGHT

'Bethan, is that you?'
'No, it's Beyonce – how did you get my number?'

Alison sighed. 'Stop messing about, Bethan. Listen, I've got something important to tell you.'

'You *must* have – it's not half seven yet. Anyway, you can tell me at the res.'

'The *res*?'

'Yes. You're not the only one making early calls. Me and Harry are meeting Rob there at half eight.'

'Bit early, isn't it? And what about Carl and the cave trolls?'

Bethan chuckled. 'Carl was off school yesterday, *and* the day before. His dad smacked him at the bonfire. Harry reckons it pulverized his brain.'

Alison giggled. 'Can you pulverize something that isn't there?'

'Never mind that, Aly. Meet us by the fence at half eight. The trolls won't come without Carl, and the workmen don't do Saturdays. Wear wellies – we get to explore the old mill at last.'

When Rob arrived at twenty five to nine, the others were waiting.

'What kept you?' demanded Harry.

Rob pulled a face. 'I was just setting off when my mobi rang. Rooney, wanting a few tips on taking free kicks.' He shrugged. 'Got to help, haven't you?'

''Course you do, Rob. Come on.'

Their old footprints curved across the mud like a gigantic bite. They walked in them, watching the trees along the shore. It was a still, cold morning with a thin mist. Nothing stirred.

'Too early for old Steve,' grunted Harry.

Rob nodded. 'Hope so. You OK, girls?'

''Course,' said Bethan. 'We're younger, not babies.'

They hauled themselves onto the shore and walked along to where they could see what was left of the mill. Bethan wasn't a baby, but she was tense. Out there was where the ghost stood. She wasn't there now, but everyone's got to be somewhere. Even ghosts. *Where is she in the daytime?* whispered a voice in Bethan's head. *Can she see us?*

'OK,' growled Harry. 'Let's do it.' They slid down the bank and sloshed towards the remains of Hopwood Mill.

Halfway, Bethan remembered something. She touched Alison's sleeve. 'What were you going to tell me, Aly?'

Alison groaned. 'I hoped you'd forgotten about that, Bethan.' She put her mouth to her friend's ear. 'Guy from the *Echo* come to our place last night. Mum and Dad were out. Tony screened your snapshot for him.'

'Oh, no!' Bethan looked stricken. 'He's not going to put it in the *paper*, is he? Mum'll go ape-shape.'

Alison shrugged. 'He says not.' She looked at

her friend. 'Tony couldn't help it. The guy practically forced him. Said he was just curious, didn't ask for a printout or anything so maybe it'll be OK.'

Bethan nodded. 'Let's hope so. And let's hope he's not curious enough to come poking about here today – this is *our* adventure.'

FORTY-NINE

'Hey look.' Harry pointed to the ground they stood on. 'There's hardly any mud here. It's cobbles, like some streets in the village.' He grinned. 'This isn't going to be as messy as I expected.'

'We're in the mill yard, I suppose,' said Bethan. 'These walls all round were the weaving sheds, and the warehouse and office and that.'

'Weird, isn't it?' breathed Rob. 'The last people to cross this yard have been dead for a hundred years. D'you think if we listen really hard, we might hear the fading echo of their clogs.'

'Oooh, Rob, *don't*.' Alison shivered. 'I'm scared

enough wondering if I'll walk round the end of a wall and bump into the ghost, without *you* starting.'

Harry laughed. 'You won't bump *into* her, Alison, you'll walk right through.'

'Shut up, Harry,' snarled Bethan. 'We're here to explore, not to tell ghost stories. What're all these heaps of rubble, d'you think?'

'They're broken stones,' said Rob. 'It'll be all the stuff that wasn't worth carting off when they demolished the place.' He kicked a lump. 'The chimney stones'd smash when it fell, wouldn't they?'

They walked about, scrambling over mounds that shifted under their feet, running their hands along the slimy tops of walls. Bethan tried to picture what it must be like here when the reservoir was full – a realm of dim green light, swaying plants and shoals of little fish. An alien place, lost to human eyes. Now the fishes were confined to the dark pool which lay in the deepest part of the reservoir.

It was Rob who made the find. He called to the others in such an odd voice that they knew he had something special before they ran to him.

The bones lay along the foot of a wall, close in, as if their owner had sought a sheltered place to sleep. There were long bones, ribs and vertebrae, and a skull so like the ones they'd seen in movies that they knew for sure it was human.

FIFTY

They gazed in silence at the bones, feeling unreal. People on TV find skeletons. Pretend detectives and real archaeologists. Kids *imagine* themselves finding skeletons during adventures, but they never actually have adventures of that sort. Or of *any* sort, really.

Rob broke the silence, more for the sake of breaking it than anything else. 'How come you girls aren't screaming?' he asked in a husky voice. 'On telly, if a woman finds a body she screams.'

Alison whispered, 'I've noticed that. Scriptwriters live in a time warp. They think we

155

still swoon at anything wilder than embroidery.'

'*I*'ll scream if you like,' volunteered Harry. 'I nearly did anyway.'

Rob shook his head. 'No it's OK, Harry, thanks.' He looked towards the shore. 'We might not be by ourselves much longer, so we better decide what we want to do.'

Alison looked at him. 'What d'you mean, *want to do*. What *can* we do?'

'Well, Alison, these are human remains. What we *ought* to do is tell the police, in case it's a murder or something. But . . .' He pulled a face. 'If we do, that's the end of our adventure. They'll put blue and white tape round and we'll never get close again.'

Bethan shook her head. 'Let's not do that, Rob. Not just yet.' She nodded towards the bones. 'This might be the ghost.'

'Well, yes it might,' agreed Rob, 'but we're not whatsit – forensic scientists. What d'you think we can actually *do*?'

'Well *I* don't know,' snapped Bethan. 'Look for clues. Take snapshots. Anything but back off the first real adventure we've ever had.'

Rob nodded. 'OK, Bethan, we'll poke about a

bit, and you can take some pics.' His eyes swept the shoreline. 'We better get a move on though – old Steve might show up anytime. And that reporter.'

FIFTY-ONE

They squatted in a semicircle round the skeleton. 'It's old,' said Harry. 'You can tell by the colour of the bones – more browny green than white.'

Bethan nodded. 'Yes, and there are no clothes. There'd be clothes if it was new. And shoes.'

Rob shook his head. 'You can't say that, Bethan. How do you know the guy wasn't naked when he fell in the water?'

'*She*,' corrected Bethan. 'We're looking at the ghost of Wilton Water, couldn't be anyone else.'

Rob snorted. 'You can't say *that* either. Ten people might have drowned in this reservoir over the years. And we don't know the difference between a lady skeleton and a man skeleton.'

'But it *is* old,' insisted Harry. 'And the police aren't interested in bodies a hundred years old or more.'

'How d'you know that?' asked Alison.

Harry sighed. 'Stands to reason, Aly. If someone murdered someone a hundred years ago, the murderer's dead too by now, isn't he? They can't stick him in jail, so what's the point?'

'We should still report it,' said Rob.

'We will,' agreed Bethan, 'when we've had our adventure.' She pulled the camera out of her jacket and aimed it at the skull. 'Smile, please.'

Rob stood up, scanned the shore. 'If we want to extend our so-called adventure past today,' he growled, 'we'll need to hide the skeleton so nobody else finds it.'

Harry looked up at him. 'How?'

'Only one way,' Rob replied. 'Stack broken stones on top of it, make it look like just another heap. Better be quick too, 'cause I think someone's coming.'

They scurried back and forth, carrying lumps of stone, stacking them like a cairn over the bones. They hadn't quite finished when Rob said, 'OK guys, that'll have to do. It's Steve, and he's got his wellies on.'

They placed a few last stones, walking crouched so the ruins hid them, then emerged and trudged in a knot towards the shore, laughing and horsing around. Steve Wood watched them scramble up the bank.

'You guys're bright and early this morning,' he greeted. 'Anything interesting out there?'

'Naw.' Rob pulled a face. 'Nothing but a bunch of old walls, Steve. We're off to do something more exciting, like watching chicken parts thaw.'

FIFTY-TWO

It started to drizzle. They headed for the bus shelter. Harry chuckled. 'Chicken parts. Where'd you get *that* one, Rob?'

Rob shrugged. 'Dunno. TV, I suppose. We can find sticks, scrape the muck off our wellies.'

There were only two buses on Saturdays. The first had gone, the other wasn't due till one o'clock. The shelter was unoccupied. They sat on the bench in their socks, working at their wellies.

'Wonder what Steve's doing,' muttered Bethan. 'I hope he doesn't find our bones.'

Her brother grinned. 'They're not *our* bones, Sis – we're still wearing those.'

Bethan scowled. 'Nobody likes a smartass, Harry.' She wasn't going to admit it, but the ghost was haunting her again. *She'll know, won't she*, murmured a voice inside her head. *She'll know we found her skeleton and didn't report it because we want an adventure. And what does she want? A proper burial for one thing, I bet. Not someone with a camera going smile please, that's for sure.* She shook her head. *I can't believe I said that.*

'He won't hang about in this stuff.' Rob nodded at the rain. 'Probably home right now, working on his latest book.'

Harry pulled a face. 'Hope you're right, Rob, but he was a postman, remember – out in all weathers.'

Alison shrugged. 'Nowt we can do about it anyway. At least we got pictures.' She nudged her friend. 'Let's have a look at 'em, Bethan.'

Bethan produced the camera, handed it to Alison.

Alison selected quick view, peered at the tiny screen. 'Hey, Beth, this is a good one,' she chirped. She was about to scroll forward when a shadow fell across her. She looked up.

The man in the raincoat smiled. 'What is it, Alison – another ghost?'

FIFTY-THREE

'Who're you?' asked Rob, before Alison could reply.

The man stuck a hand out. 'Stan Fox. And you?'

Rob hesitated, then took the hand. 'Rob Hattersley.' He gestured to the others. 'Alison Crabtree, Harry and Bethan Midgley. How do you know about the ghost?'

The man grinned. 'Saw it on-screen at this young lady's house.' He nodded towards Alison.

'Oh, yeah.' Alison nodded. 'Our Tony showed you. He wasn't supposed to.'

Fox pulled a face. 'Sorry. I promised not to

164

print anything and I haven't, but I must admit I'm curious.'

'Curiosity killed the cat,' growled Rob.

Bethan thought this sounded rude, but the man only smiled. 'Hasn't killed the Fox though – not yet anyway.' He nodded at the camera. 'You going to let me see, Alison?'

Alison shrugged. 'It's Bethan's camera, she took the pics. You better ask her.'

Fox looked at Bethan. 'I bet you're the one who snapped the ghost, aren't you? It's a terrific shot – near professional.' He smiled. 'But you don't want to be famous, right?'

Bethan stared at her socks. 'I don't want my mum to know I went up the res at night,' she mumbled. 'That's all.'

'Aaah!' Fox nodded. 'I understand, Bethan, I had a mum like that.' He smiled. 'OK then, same promise – whatever's on your camera, it won't find its way into the *Echo*.'

'And you won't tell the police,' added Bethan without looking up.

'The police?' said Fox, surprised. 'You mean you've got something they'd be interested in?'

Bethan nodded. 'Maybe, but this is our

adventure, right? We found it and we're investigating. We don't want blue and white tape cutting us out. Grown-ups always cut kids out of interesting stuff.'

'Yes, but still.' Fox cleared his throat. 'I think I'd better have a look, Alison, if you don't mind.'

'All right.' She put the camera into the reporter's hand. 'But you promised, remember.'

FIFTY-FOUR

The stones the kids had heaped up looked just like the other heaps to them, but it didn't fool Steve Wood. As Fox gaped at the camera image of the skeleton, the squatting historian was gaping at the bones themselves.

Nothing but a bunch of old walls, eh? He chuckled. *Crafty young devils.* He gazed at the discoloured skull. *How long's this been here, I wonder? Quite a while I'd say, though I'm no expert.* He pulled a face. *I know a lass who is, though. I wonder . . .*

He stood up, frowning, trying to recall any report in recent years of an unexplained disappearance from the area. As a local historian he'd remember, but nothing came to mind. *Of course* ... He smiled faintly. *There was Hettie Daynes, but that was way back in 1885. Surely* ...

He squatted again, inserted a hand and drew out a short, thin bone. Like Stan Fox, Steve was a curious man. Questions were forming in his mind, one after another. *How long has this skeleton been here? Is it female? Could it possibly be that of Hettie Daynes? Was Hettie even a real person and if so, could I unearth any facts about her? If I give this bone to my friend at the university, will she be able to date the remains for me?*

And most importantly, ought I even to be thinking about making a project out of this, instead of reporting the skeleton to the police?

Without noticing, he'd started to put the chunks of stone back where he found them. Like the children, he was keen to investigate the matter himself. Like them, he knew that once the authorities were told, he'd find himself shoved to one side.

Of course, he reminded himself, *the kids might decide to report it – they found it after all.* He shrugged, stood up and began picking his way towards dry land, the bone in a pocket of his waxed jacket.

Hope I can persuade Avril to do the science.

FIFTY-FIVE

Fox handed the camera back to Alison. 'So, what do you kids intend to do about this?'

Rob looked at him. 'We're going to investigate.'

'How?'

Rob shrugged. 'Dig about in the mud, see what turns up.'

The reporter smiled. 'Such as?'

'Well . . . something that'll tell us who she was. Like . . . I dunno, a ring or a bracelet or something.'

'She?' queried Fox. 'Why d'you think it's a woman?'

''S obvious,' said Bethan. 'It's the ghost, isn't it?'

Fox chuckled. 'If you know that, why d'you need clues?'

'We want to prove she's Hettie Daynes.'

Fox looked puzzled. 'What – as in *daft as Hettie Daynes*, you mean?'

Bethan nodded. 'Yes.'

The reporter shook his head. 'But she's not real, Bethan. It's just an expression people use – *daft as Hettie Daynes*. It's like *daft as a brush*, or *daft as a box of frogs*.'

'No it isn't,' snapped Harry. 'Hettie Daynes was real. She was our mum's great, great auntie. She vanished.'

Fox frowned at the boy. 'Are you winding me up, lad?'

Harry shook his head. 'No, I'm not.'

'He isn't,' put in Alison. 'His mum asked me not to go as Hettie Daynes to the Hallowe'en Hop. That's why I went as the ghost.'

'But . . . ?' The reporter looked bewildered. 'You think they're the same person – isn't that what you're saying?'

Alison nodded. 'Yes.'

171

'So, isn't going as the ghost the same as going as Hettie Daynes? I don't understand.'

'No.' Bethan shook her head. 'It's not the same, Mr Fox. See – Aly was going to go in torn clothes, dirty and crying, 'cause that's what Hettie was like before she disappeared. She wouldn't be wet. The ghost's wet because she comes up out of the water – well, you've seen the snapshot.'

'Budge up a bit, Rob,' growled Fox. Rob shuffled along the bench and the reporter sat down, leaning forward to see Bethan. 'But your mum didn't mind Alison going as the ghost?'

'No, 'cause she says the ghost *isn't* her great, great auntie. In fact she doesn't believe there *is* any ghost. She says it's just a local legend.'

'Ah.' Fox nodded. 'So she hasn't seen your snapshot?'

''Course not. I told you – she'd kill me if she knew I was even *at* the res that night.'

'Right.' Fox sat quietly for a bit, frowning at the concrete floor. Then he roused himself and said, 'Yes, all right. We *ought* to tell the police about the bones and it might come to that in the end, but we'll leave it for the moment. Let me know if you find anything interesting.' He stood up, looked down at them. 'Investigate, but please follow these three rules. One: stick together. Nobody is to be at the reservoir by herself or himself at any time. Two: keep away from the water at all times. It's very deep, and very cold. And three: don't disturb the bones. Dig round them if you must, but leave them as they lie – it might be important later on.'

They watched him walk away, then pulled on their wellies and left the shelter.

FIFTY-SIX

Fox drove back to the *Echo* building in Rawton. He got a coffee from the dispenser in the newsroom, carried it to his cubicle and shut the door. He sat, sipping and staring at the wall.

Hettie Daynes. Alison gives Bill that name at the school. Says she thinks it's the ghost's name. Bill jots it down, Reginald Hopwood overhears and tells him not to put it in the paper. Threatens him.

And before that, a couple of Saturdays ago, Reginald has his knickers in a twist about sightseers at Wilton Water. Wants security stepped up. A piece in the paper wouldn't do any harm, he says.

Now it turns out there's a human skeleton at the reservoir, and a bunch of inquisitive kids have found it. A guy with a suspicious mind might almost think Hopwood knew something was there.

The reporter drained the styrofoam cup, crunched it in his fist and lobbed it into the wastepaper basket. Ridiculous of course – how could Hopwood know any such thing? How could *anyone*? The skeleton had been under six feet of water, probably for donkey's years. Nobody could've known it was there.

Hettie Daynes, though. Fox scribbled the name on a pad, gazed at it. Wrote *daft as* in front of it. A local expression that turns out to refer to an actual person who vanished. A great, great auntie. So, a long time ago then. He frowned.

Suppose the kids're right, and the skeleton belongs to this vanished girl, Hettie Daynes. Why would Councillor Hopwood not want her name printed in the Echo? *Is it possible he knows something about her – something he'd rather keep hidden? Bit far-fetched, but hard to account for his peculiar behaviour otherwise.*

Some people would put it down to sheer coincidence, but I'm not some people.

I'm Curiosity Fox.

FIFTY-SEVEN

Carl studied his reflection in his parents' bedroom mirror. The swelling had gone down,
but his ear and cheek were still tinged with blue.

'Pig.' He glowered at the image of his father in
the wedding photo. He wasn't supposed to be in
this room, but the councillor was out. And so, for
once, was his wife. There was a civic reception
for some overseas visitors at Rawton Town Hall,
and the partners of councillors were expected to
attend.

Carl picked up the photo and held it close to
his face. 'Fat, puffed-up, red-faced bullying pig,'
he snarled. 'Why don't you stand on top of the

London Eye and lose your balance?' In fact, his father was neither fat nor red-faced in the picture. Years of soft living had thickened the racing-snake figure, broken tiny blood vessels in the face and shortened the temper, to produce the Reginald his son and heir despised.

He put the photo down and left the room. There was one place in the house even more off limits to him – the councillor's office. It was an attic room under the slope of the roof. Reginald had his computer there, and a steel filing cabinet which was always locked. It was also the room where the Hopwood family archive was stored.

It was his father's pride and joy, this archive. It consisted of trunkful after trunkful of letters, photographs, certificates, invitations, bills of fare, copies of speeches, illuminated addresses, medals, trophies, and badges, hats and jackets from the uniforms of forgotten orders and disbanded regiments. They were symbols of the distinguished lives of Hopwood ancestors, stretching all the way back to the eighteenth century and the birth of Josiah Hopwood, builder of Hopwood Mill and founder of the family fortune.

Reginald was rightly proud of his ancestors, and treasured these mouldering testimonials to their glory. He intended going through all this stuff eventually, getting it into some sort of logical order, but hadn't got round to it yet.

Which is a pity, because the archive contained an item which would blow his world apart.

FIFTY-EIGHT

'Hi, Avril – thanks for coming at such short notice.' The historian stood aside to let his friend enter, then closed the door. 'Coffee or tea? Kettle's on.'

It was seven o'clock Saturday evening. The woman smiled, nodded. 'Coffee'll be fine, thanks.' She sat down in an armchair. Steve went through to the kitchen. 'So,' said Avril, when they were settled with coffee. 'What's all the excitement about, Steve?'

'Bones.'

'Bones?' The pathologist looked at him through the steam from her cup. Steve nodded.

'Human bones, exposed by the draining of Wilton Water and found today by a bunch of kids from the village.'

'Wow!' exclaimed Avril. 'You sure they're human?'

Steve nodded. 'Absolutely. Complete skeleton, virtually.'

'You've told the police, of course.'

'Uh – no.' He smiled at her expression. 'They're old bones, Avril. I don't know *how* old, of course, which is where you come in.'

'Oh it is, is it?' The woman blew on her coffee, took a sip. 'I'm not sure I ought to get involved.' She frowned. 'It's got to be an offence surely, keeping something like this to yourself?'

The historian shrugged. 'I dunno. Anyway . . .' He grinned. 'When did *you* start worrying about what's an offence and what isn't? Last *I* heard, you were still the same old maverick.' He produced the bone he'd removed from the site. 'Here. Lighten up and tell me what you think.'

The woman examined the bone, turning it this way and that under the electric light. Steve watched her over the rim of his cup till she looked up. 'Well, it's a clavicle. Old, as you said, but I can't tell how old by just looking. I'd have to do tests.'

'Will you do 'em for me, Avril?'

She pulled a face. 'I suppose so.' She looked at him. 'It'd help if I could see the rest of it, Steve.'

He nodded. 'No prob. Were you doing anything special tomorrow?'

FIFTY-NINE

Eight o'clock on Monday morning. The Hopwoods at breakfast. A silent, awkward meal. Felicity avoids talking to her husband, who tends to be savage in the mornings at the best of times. As for Carl, he's got a secret he can't share with either of them. He found it Saturday night, rooting in the archive. The ink's faded and the writing's hard to read, but he suspects it's seriously weird. It's in the backpack he takes to school. He stares at his soggy cornflakes, imagining what would happen if his father suddenly took it into his head to look through his son's stuff.

Nightmare.

The councillor's mobi chimes. He swears, slams down the butter knife, stabs the talk button. 'Hopwood.'

'Ah . . . morning, Councillor. You won't know me, but I voted for you last—'

'Hang on.' He shoves back his chair, gets up and leaves the room, closing the door behind him.

Mother and son exchange looks. Neither speaks, but they're thinking the same thought. *Councillor Hopwood, busy man. Can't even eat breakfast in peace, he's so indispensable – and oh, how he loves it.*

He's in full flow, they can hear him faintly through the door. After ten minutes he comes back.

'Who was that?' asks Felicity as her husband resumes his seat. She ought to know better.

'None of your damn business.' He sweeps the toast rack off the table with the back of his hand. 'Cold, as usual.' The slices skitter across the carpet. '*That's* your business, Felicity, if only you'd attend to it.'

Carl's hands curl into fists on the tablecloth.

You wait, he thinks. *You think you're so great, nobody can touch you, but you're wrong. Just you wait.*

SIXTY

In a cellar under the *Echo* building lay the newspaper's own library. It had no books, but there were copies of every edition of the *Echo* going back to the very first, printed in the spring of 1865. The papers were bound up between hard covers, each volume holding one year's editions.

There was a broad, battered table and an old swivel chair. On the chair slumped Steve Wood, looking like a sack of spuds. He'd been here more than three hours, and had leafed through two hundred and twenty copies of the paper. On the table, open, lay the volume for 1887. The

185

historian's right hand rested on an inside page of an edition printed in November of that year. The library was poorly lit and hopelessly old-fashioned. Anywhere else, everything would be on disk or microfiche and he'd probably have found what he'd been looking for in minutes. Nevertheless he was feeling pretty pleased with himself as he read this:

A NEW SIMILE

The attention of your correspondent has been drawn to a rare phenomenon: namely, the rise of an apparently new simile, whose place and approximate year of birth are actually known. The simile, overheard in more than one conversation among factory hands at Wilton, runs thus: As daft as Hettie Daynes. It is applied to any person perceived to have committed a particularly foolish or imprudent act, and arises out of events in the village a few years ago, when it seems an apparently demented young woman was observed by many, weeping and rending her garments.

The origins of many similes in common use are lost in the mists of time, and it is interesting to speculate as to whether this one will spread beyond the boundaries of Wilton, and of the present century, to issue from the mouths of persons totally ignorant of the circumstance out of which it arose.

Steve Wood scribbled a note, closed the volume and replaced it on its shelf. *Events in the village a few years ago*. He sighed. *I wonder why they didn't make the local paper, these events?*

SIXTY-ONE

The Feathers, Thursday lunch time. Councillor Reginald Hopwood and journalist Stan Fox at their usual table. Fox lifted his tankard. 'Cheers, Councillor.'

'Cheers, Stan.' Hopwood sipped his ale, feeling nervous. Would his companion mention the reservoir, his threat to the photographer, *Hettie Daynes?* Was he going to ask awkward questions, or had he not noticed anything unusual?

Curiosity Fox noticed *everything*, including the councillor's unease. He had questions, but didn't know quite how to put them.

'So, anything new?' he began. It was the one

question he always asked.

'Don't think so, Stan.' Hopwood kept his tone and expression neutral. 'Quiet, I'd call it.' He smiled. '*Too* quiet for you, probably – I know how you guys like a bit of sensation.'

'We *do*, Councillor.' Fox gazed into his tankard. 'Especially me.' He looked up. 'I make no bones about it.'

Was it his imagination, or did his companion pale slightly at those last words?

As Fox and Hopwood fenced at The Feathers, Steve Wood ploughed through old census rolls at Rawton town hall till he found this:

Prince's Street. No. 8.

Ebor Daynes, textile operative.

Alexis Daynes (wife) spinner.

Children: Albert, 17 yrs. Carter's mate.

Hettie, 16 yrs. Textile operative.

Henry, 11 yrs.

Margaret, 10yrs.

Mary, 8yrs.

Harold, 6 yrs.

Dorothy, 7 months.

The historian smiled and nodded, jotting in his notebook:

Hettie, 16 yrs. Textile operative.

SIXTY-TWO

Friday morning, Steve's phone played a bar from the 1812 Overture. He thumbed the green stud. 'Hi, Avril.'

'Morning, Steve.'

'How're you?'

'I'm OK. I pinched some lab time last night, ran the tests.'

'Great. And . . . ?'

'The bones're a century old, give or take twenty years or so. And the skeleton's female.'

'Tremendous! That plonks it right where I hoped it'd be. Thanks, Avril, I mean it.'

'There's something else, Steve.'

191

'What?'

'Well – one of the bits we picked up Sunday . . . it's not part of her, whoever she was.'

'Not part of her . . . what d'you mean?'

'It belongs to an infant. A very young infant.'

'You mean *two* people drowned?'

'Sort of. I can't remember exactly where this particular bone was in relation to the skeleton, but I think the child was in the womb.'

'Ah.'

'I could probably confirm this by taking another look on site.'

'OK, Avril. Tomorrow or Sunday, whichever's best for you.'

Rawton Secondary School. Afternoon break. To avoid going outside in the drizzle, Carl Hopwood hid in the boys' lavatories.

Carl liked to read on the lavatory. A lot of guys do. He fished from his pack the diary he'd found in the archive at home, and settled on the seat.

The diary had a lock, which Carl had forced. Its jacket was of scuffed leather, red once, now faded to a brownish pink. The year 1885 was embossed on it in tarnished gilt. On the first page in a fine copperplate hand, were these words:

The Journal of Stanton Farley Hopwood.

Stanton Hopwood had been Carl's great grand-father. He had died in 1939.

A musty smell rose as Carl turned the thin, foxed leaves, looking for October 6th. He'd read the entry a couple of times before. It was the one that had got his attention in the first place:

Accosted by H. this afternoon while crossing the yard. Strident. Told her be quiet, I was making plans and would speak to her soon. Plans! I have no plans. Would that I had.

Boring stuff followed, until this on the thirteenth:

Waylaid again, this time perilously close to Father's office. H. threatening to tell her mother unless I name the day. Silly little fool surely can't imagine Father's plans for me include marriage to one of his hands?

Carl smiled. He was only thirteen, but he pretty much knew what was what. Stanton Farley Hopwood had been a *very* naughty boy, and Carl doubted whether Councillor Reginald Hopwood (busy man) would want this to get out, even after all this time.

SIXTY-THREE

'Your glossy's come,' said Norah Crabtree,
when Alison got in from school. 'It's on the
kitchen table.' Norah was watching TV as usual.

Alison found the brown envelope under a
mountain of clothes awaiting her mother's iron. It
was addressed to her, but Mum had opened
it anyway. She pulled out Bill's photo.

'Oh, *sweet*,' she whispered, gazing at it. 'Am I a
genius or what? That *skirt*, the way it hangs. The
hair, the eyeliner – *everything*. And just *look* how
my feet stand out white against the black of that
puddle. It didn't look *half* this good in the paper.'

She spun on one foot, laughing, holding up the

195

photograph. 'No *wonder* old Hopwood couldn't resist giving me the prize!'

She scampered upstairs, punched in Bethan's number. 'Beth, my glossy came. Wait till you see it. I look *exactly* like the ghost we saw the night you slept over, *and* I've already decided what I'm going as next year.' She laughed with excitement. 'I'm going as our *skeleton*!'

She waited for her friend's reaction, but instead a voice said, 'Who *is* this? Alison? This is Bethan's mother. Bethan's in the bathroom, and it seems she'll have some explaining to do when she comes out. Thank you for calling. Goodbye.'

SIXTY-FOUR

Bethan came into the kitchen. She'd changed out of her school clothes. Harry flashed her a warning look, which she failed to understand. She looked at her mother.

'Did I hear my phone just now?' Christa was stirring something in a pan. When she turned, Bethan saw the look on her face. 'What . . . is something *wrong*, Mum?'

Christa nodded. '*I* think so, Bethan. You *did* hear your phone. Alison Crabtree called. She wants you to know her glossy's come, and that she looks exactly like the ghost you and she saw the night you slept over.'

Bethan's face fell. 'Ah. Yes. Right.' Her mind started to race, but it failed to turn up anything she might usefully say.

'Oh,' continued Christa, 'and she's already decided what she intends to go as *next* year – I assume she's talking about the Hallowe'en Hop. She's going to go as *our skeleton*, whatever that means.' She eyed her daughter narrowly. 'I suppose *you* know what it means, Bethan?'

Bethan hung her head. 'Yes, Mum.'

'Well? What is *our skeleton*?'

'It's . . . we found it, Mum. At the old mill.'

'*What* old mill? What are you talking about, child?'

Harry broke in. 'She means the mill at Wilton Water, Mum. Hopwood Mill. There's a skeleton. Human. We found it.'

His mother stared. '*When*, Harry? When did all this happen, and why am I the last to know about it?'

'It was last Saturday,' said Harry. 'The eighth. We didn't tell you because . . . because it's our adventure.'

'And because we think it's Hettie Daynes,' added Bethan.

'Whoa, just a minute.' Christa sank onto a chair, gazed at her children. 'It sounds to me as though you've both been practically *living* by that reservoir, in spite of the fact that I've asked you to stay away from it, and in defiance of warnings at school *and* in the *Echo* about its being dangerous.'

'We've been really, really careful, Mum,' murmured Bethan. 'Mr Wood and Mr Fox *both* told us what to do, and we've taken notice.'

Christa looked at her. 'Does Steve Wood know about this skeleton?'

Bethan shook her head. 'I don't know, Mum. *We* didn't show it to him.' She tried on a smile. 'Grown-ups spoil everything.'

'And who's Mr Fox?'

'He's the chief reporter on the *Echo*, Mum,' said Harry.

His mother nodded. 'Yes, of course. And what about him – has *he* seen the skeleton?'

'He's seen our snapshots of it.'

'There are *snapshots*?'

'Yes, Mum. D'you want to see them?'

Christa covered her face with her hands, shook her head. 'What *I* want, Harry, is for my children *not* to be leading a secret life, involving ghosts and skeletons and reservoirs. I want the *police* to deal with any skeletons that might be around. I want priests or psychic investigators to cope with ghosts. I want my children to lead dull, unadventurous lives *here*, at number eight, Leaf Street.' She dropped her hands. 'Since you ask me what I want, Harry – *that's* what I want.'

SIXTY-FIVE

Saturday morning. Fox came out of the *Echo* building and practically bumped into Steve Wood. 'Now then, Steve.' Wood had occasional pieces printed in the *Echo*, and was a frequent user of the newspaper's library.

'Stan.' Wood grinned. 'Just off to cover the Rovers match, are you?' Rawton Rovers were away to Lincoln that day.

'Nah.' The reporter shook his head. 'Not my interest, mate. Colleague of mine's a fan, I let *him* cover the Rovers. I'm poking about in what you might call a local mystery.'

The historian smiled. 'Sounds more like

201

my sort of thing.'

Fox nodded. 'I suppose it is, Steve. It concerns Wilton Water.'

Wood looked at him. 'That's a coincidence. *I'm* researching a fascinating piece of local history at the reservoir too.'

Fox smiled. 'There's no such thing as coincidence, Steve. Would your bit of history involve a skeleton?'

Wood looked startled. 'How the heck did *you* know, Stan? I thought it was my secret. Well . . .' He pulled a face. 'Mine and the kids who found it.'

The reporter nodded. 'I met some kids last Saturday in the bus shelter. They had a camera. Showed me snapshots they'd taken of a skeleton, in the old mill.'

'Yeah,' sighed Steve. 'That's where it is.' He kicked a pebble into the road. 'I was at your place Monday, looking for stuff on Hettie Daynes.' He looked at Fox. 'You know, the mad lass who disappeared? The bones're about a century old. I thought there was a slim chance they might be hers.'

Fox nodded. 'Find anything?'

'Nothing till a couple of years after she's

supposed to have vanished. Then it was just a piece about the saying, *daft as Hettie Daynes*. Didn't help at all.' He grinned. 'Found her in the census records though. Mill girl, lived on Prince's Street in Wilton. One of seven kids.'

The reporter shrugged. 'Not unusual in those days.' He pulled a face. 'Anyway, the age of the bones scuppers *my* theory.'

Wood shook his head. 'Sorry, mate. What *was* your theory?'

The reporter snorted. 'Daren't tell you, Steve, it involved a local resident. Sue the pants off me if he got wind of it.'

Wood frowned. 'What made you think . . . ?'

'Let's just say somebody seemed to have a keen interest in keeping nosy parkers away from Wilton Water, so when those kids showed me their snapshots, it occurred to me there might have been a murder.' He grinned ruefully. 'A *recent* one, I mean.'

'Ah.' The historian thought for a moment. 'There *might* have been a murder though,' he murmured, 'a hundred years ago, because' – he looked at Fox – 'the skeleton's female, and the lass was expecting a baby.'

SIXTY-SIX

'Mum?'

'What is it, Carl?' Felicity slid an enormous steak pie into the oven. Reginald was at the Wilton Community Centre, making himself available to his public. *My monthly surgery*, he called it, and it always left him both ravenous and ratty. The pie would fix the ravenous part: only time would fix the ratty.

'What's a hand?'

'A hand?' She closed the oven door and straightened up. 'Whatever d'you mean, dear? You know perfectly well what a hand is.'

'No.' Carl shook his head. 'I mean a hand as in,

*silly little fool surely can't imagine my father's plans
for me include marriage to one of his hands.'*

Felicity looked puzzled. 'What's *that* from, Carl
– something you're reading at school?'

Carl nodded. 'Yes, Mum, I read it at school.'

'Well.' His mother frowned. 'It sounds to me
like Victorian literature. *Is* it?'

'Yes, it was written in Victorian times.'

'I don't recognize it – what's the title?'

'A journal.'

Felicity shrugged. 'Can't say I've heard of it,
but in those days factory workers were known as
hands.' She smiled sadly. 'I suppose that was the
only part of them their employers cared about –
the part that did the work. Anyway, it sounds to
me as though the character in your book is a
young man who's become involved with a girl – a
factory hand. His family is probably from
a higher class than hers, so his father won't want
him to marry her.' She smiled. 'Am I close?'

Carl nodded. 'Pretty much, Mum, yeah.' He
left the kitchen, went to his room and took the
diary out of his backpack. He lay on the bed,
propped by pillows, and read on.

October seventeenth:

She weeps around the village: how can it not come out? I contemplate drastic measures. If I'm driven to act on them, she's only herself to blame.

October nineteenth:

Desperation. We're to meet at the mill at nine p.m. tomorrow when, God willing, all will be resolved.

October twentieth (written in a shaky hand):

It is done. I do most fervently wish it had not proved necessary, but she drove me to it. Soon the rising waters will conceal my crime, but will prove insufficient to the cleansing of my soul, upon which the Lord have mercy.

'I've *seen* you, haven't I?' breathed Carl. 'Bonfire Night, at the res, standing on nothing. No *wonder* you gave me that look.'

He couldn't stop shivering.

SIXTY-SEVEN

Sunday morning at eight Leaf Street. After a hard week at the minimarket Christa was sleeping late, her dreams haunted by snapshots of bones and spectres. Harry and Bethan crept about downstairs, making breakfast, hoping Mum might wake in a better frame of mind.

The phone rang.

'Drat!' Harry strode across the kitchen and picked up. 'Yes?' He hoped it hadn't disturbed his mother.

'Who am I speaking to?' A man's voice.

'Harry Midgley, who's this?'

'Fox, the *Echo*. We met at the bus shelter. Is your mother there?'

'She's having a lie-in Mr Fox. Can *I* help?'

'I really need to speak to your mum, Harry. It's about the skeleton, and Hettie Daynes.'

'Mum doesn't like talking about Hettie Daynes.'

'I know,' said Fox, 'but I fancy she'll be interested in what I have to say. I know I promised but things have come to light, it's gone beyond a kids' adventure. Tell her I'll call round sometime after two.'

'Who was that?' asked Bethan, pouring milk on her cornflakes.

Harry pulled a face. 'Stan Fox. You know, the reporter? He's coming to see Mum. Wants to talk about Hettie Daynes and the skeleton.'

'But . . .' Bethan slopped milk on the tablecloth.

'I *know*, I know. He pulled the grown-up act – *you kids don't understand these things*. Typical.' He tossed his sister a cloth.

SIXTY-EIGHT

'**M**s Midgley – thanks for seeing me. And for this.' Fox raised his coffee cup.

Christa shrugged. 'I don't consider I had a choice, Mr Fox. You invited yourself while I slept.'

The reporter smiled ruefully. 'That's absolutely true, Ms Midgley. I hope you'll feel my rudeness was justified when you've heard what I have to say.'

Christa frowned at Fox in the other armchair. She'd sent Harry and Bethan upstairs on his arrival. 'My son tells me it's to do with my great, great aunt.' She shook her head. 'There are things in families – highly personal things – which members prefer to keep inside the family. The brief, tragic story of Hettie Daynes is a case in point.'

'I understand, believe me.' Fox drank some coffee, returned his cup to its saucer. 'The thing is, Ms Midgley, Steve Wood and I have reason to believe the bones uncovered at Wilton Water may well be those of your ancestor, and that something dreadful might have happened to her.'

Christa looked at him. 'You also believe my daughter took a snapshot of a ghost, so you'll forgive me if I'm not that impressed by what you *believe*, Mr Fox.'

The reporter nodded. 'Spirit photos were always a grey area, Ms Midgley,' he conceded, 'but please hear me out.' He finished his coffee, set cup and saucer on the table she'd placed between them. 'Your great, great aunt disappeared in 1885 after behaving strangely for a time, is that right?'

Christa nodded. 'Something like that. I'm not sure of the year.'

'It was 1885 – the year the reservoir filled up and Hopwood Mill disappeared.'

Christa met his gaze. 'And the bones were found in what's left of the mill. I think I can see where you're going with this, Mr Fox. You think Hettie Daynes committed suicide in the mill where she'd worked, because she was out of her mind.'

The reporter shook his head. 'I'm afraid I think something far worse than that, Ms Midgley.' He looked Christa in the eye. 'Hettie was expecting a baby, wasn't she?'

'Was she?' Christa held his gaze. 'And that's the icing on your cake, isn't it? You can splash it all over the front page: SHRINKING RES REVEALS VICTORIAN SCANDAL – HETTIE DAYNES WAS WILTON WANTON. It might even get you a job on a *real* newspaper.'

'Ouch!' Fox looked hurt. 'You certainly have a very low opinion of *me*.' He shook his head. 'It's not *your* family secret I'm investigating, Ms Midgley. If I'm right, there's a family with a far more shameful one.' He looked at Christa. 'It might well involve murder.'

'*Murder?*' cried Christa. '*Wh*ose murder? Are you saying . . . ?'

The reporter shook his head again. 'I'm not

saying anything,' he murmured. 'Not yet. The matter is under investigation. Hard evidence is scarce.'

He stood up. 'The young woman who left her bones at Hopwood Mill was pregnant, Ms Midgley. More than one reluctant father has solved his embarrassing little problem by disposing of mother and child in one go, and what better spot to choose than a mill that's about to disappear for ever?' He smiled thinly. 'What people tend to forget is, *nothing*'s for ever.'

SIXTY-NINE

Monday, before the bell. Rob gaped. 'So your mum knows *everything*, sucker – we've no secret any more?'

Harry shook his head. 'Sorry, mate. Alison Crabtree blabbed on the phone before she knew who'd picked up.'

'What a dipstick. And Stan Fox went back on his promise?'

'Yeah. Says it's gone beyond a kids' game.'

'Typical adult.'

'That's what *I* said.'

'So what'll your mum do – tell the police?'

Harry shrugged. 'Dunno. She says if the

skeleton *is* her great, great auntie, she wants to give it a proper burial.'

'What – so the ghost can like, rest? Stop haunting Wilton Water?'

'No, not that. She refuses to believe in the ghost, even though she's seen the snapshot.'

'What about Fox then? Will *he* go to the police now, d'you think?'

Harry shook his head. 'Don't think so. Him and Steve Wood have got together. They think they're looking at an old murder.'

'They think Hettie Daynes was *murdered*?'

'They think the *skeleton* was murdered – they can't prove it's Hettie.'

'Hey up,' warned Rob. 'Troubles come in threes, here's number two.' Carl Hopwood approached rapidly, with a face on him like a slapped bum. He came alone, so Rob risked a wind-up. 'Cheer up, Hopwood – it might never happen.'

'Shut your face, Hattersley.' Carl grabbed a fistful of Rob's hoodie, slammed him against the wall. 'What you done with my book?'

'Book?' gasped Rob. '*What* book? Don't tell me you've learned to *read*, Hopwood.'

Carl ignored the jibe. 'You *know* what book. It was in the bog, on the sill. I went back for it three minutes later and it had gone. Nigel saw you go in.'

Rob shook his head. 'I don't know what you're talking about, Carl, honest. *I* didn't see any book. Why would I want your book?'

The bully relaxed his grip, stepped back. 'Well *someone* must have pinched it,' he choked. His eyes filled up. 'My dad'll *kill* me if I don't get it back.' He turned and blundered away, half-blind with tears.

'Poor old Carl,' murmured Harry. 'Must've raided the councillor's library without asking. It'll be Bonfire Night all over again when his great pink self finds out.' He smiled. 'I almost feel sorry for him.'

Rob shook his head. '*I* don't.' He patted his pack. 'In fact I've got his rotten book in here.'

'You haven't!' gasped Harry. 'What if he'd searched it, Rob?'

Rob shrugged. 'Well then he'd've got it back, wouldn't he?' He grinned. 'We'll check it out in maths, see what's so vitally important.'

SEVENTY

Wilton Primary, Monday morning assembly. Miss Gadd on the platform.

'Good morning, children.'

'Good morning Miss Gadd. Good morning everybody.'

'Now.' The headteacher smiled, rubbed her hands together. 'Today is a very special day for our school. Can anybody in Year One tell us *why* it's special?' Her eyes scanned the upturned, mostly stunned faces of the ankle-biters. A blond dumpling raised her hand.

'Yes, Tabitha?'

'Miss, our Fluffy's had four kittens.'

Miss Gadd smiled. 'That's exciting news, Tabitha, but there's something else. Something about our *playground*?'

The heavy clue produced a crop of swaying hands. 'Yes, Lucy?'

'Miss, the new . . . stuff. The workmen.'

'Very good, Lucy. Well done.' The Head extended her smile to include the whole assembly. 'This morning, workmen will come to our school with diggers and trucks and all sorts of exciting, noisy things. They'll be here all week I expect, rattling the windows and reversing all over the place, installing a lovely safe area for us to play on.' She adjusted her expression to grave. 'When they've gone, taking their machines and their mess with them, our playground will be the safest place in Wilton. But while they're here, it will not. It will be dirty and dangerous.' She lifted her gaze to the back of the hall, where the teachers were sitting. 'Why all this couldn't be done during the holidays I don't know, but still.'

The teachers murmured, nodded.

Miss Gadd continued. 'This means that today, and for the rest of this week, playtimes will be

217

indoors. *Where* will playtimes be, Bethan Midgley?'

'Miss, indoors.' *Why pick on me*, thought Bethan.

'That is correct.' The Head looked fierce. 'I don't want to catch *anyone* outside, unless a class is out with its teacher. Have I made myself perfectly plain?'

Alison whispered in Bethan's ear. 'She just *is* perfectly plain.' Bethan stifled a giggle. Alison wasn't her favourite person just now. If she was smart enough to make cracks about the Head, why hadn't she the wit to ask who was on the other end of the phone?

SEVENTY-ONE

First period, maths with Trigger, whose name was actually Mr Rogers. He was on the far side of the room, helping a group working with pyramids. Rob and Harry had Carl's diary folded inside the geometry text they were supposed to be studying.

'Listen to *this*,' hissed Rob. '*October nineteenth: Desperation. We're to meet at the mill at nine p.m. tomorrow when, God willing, all will be resolved.*'

'Crikey!' gasped Harry.

Trigger glanced across. 'I'm glad you're finding the properties of cones so thrilling, Midgley, but *do* try to express your excitement in a less exuberant manner, there's a good lad.'

'Yes, sir,' said Harry.

'And this,' murmured Rob, as Trigger returned to his pyramids. 'October twentieth: *It is done. I do most fervently wish it had not proved necessary, but she drove me to it.*'

'He *killed* her, didn't he?' whispered Harry. 'Carl's great grandad or whatever *killed Mum's auntie.*'

'Sssh!' Rob looked at Trigger, who hadn't heard. 'There's more, mate: *Soon the rising waters will conceal my crime, but will prove insufficient to the cleansing of my soul, upon which the Lord have mercy.*'

'Wow.' Harry shook his head. 'So the skeleton *is* Hettie Daynes. I'll have to show Mum this diary, I don't know what she'll do.' He looked at Rob. 'You can't get a dead guy tried for murder, can you?'

Rob pulled a face. 'No, but think what it'll do to our mighty councillor if it gets out – no wonder Carl's practically messing himself.'

Trigger straightened up. 'Tell you what, you two. Why don't the rest of us take a little break while you demonstrate your absorbing discovery for us on the board?'

SEVENTY-TWO

'Newsroom, Fox speaking.'

'It's Christa Midgley, Mr Fox. I've been going over and over what you told me yesterday. If what you suspect is true – if my great, great aunt *was* murdered, and if somebody's known this all along, ought they not to be exposed? I mean, I *know* whatever happened was too long ago for the police to get involved, but can't you put something in the paper – a piece by Steve Wood, perhaps?'

The reporter shook his head, though she couldn't see. 'I can understand your frustration, Ms Midgley – your *anger*, I suppose I should say

221

– but as I pointed out yesterday, there's no hard evidence. The fact that I *suspect* a certain family doesn't mean they're guilty.' He sighed. 'I daren't expose the *Echo* to legal action for defamation. That's why Steve and I are still investigating.'

'What about my ancestor's remains?' asked Christa. 'I want to arrange a proper burial for them, but I *don't* want to remove evidence which might be important later.'

'No,' said Fox. 'I think we need the bones to lie where they were found, Ms Midgley. For now anyway.'

'But what if somebody *else* stumbles across them – the workmen, for instance?'

'I think that's unlikely. Steve tells me they're under a cairn, one of several at the site, and the work is to the western end of the reservoir. There's a slight risk, I suppose, but it's one we'll have to take.' He thought for a moment, then added, 'There's one thing you *can* do, Ms Midgley.'

'Oh – what's that?'

'See that the kids stay away. Some stickybeak notices *them* poking about, he'll wonder what the big attraction is.'

'They won't be poking about,' promised Christa. 'They'll be lucky if they set foot on a pavement outside school hours.'

'Glad you're not *my* mum,' chuckled Fox. 'I'll keep you posted. 'Bye.'

SEVENTY-THREE

Monday tea time. Christa preparing the meal, Bethan helping. Harry came through the door.

'Mum.'

'What is it, Harry?'

'Something to show you.'

'I'm rinsing rice, love, hands're wet, can it wait?'

Harry shook his head. 'You'll want to see this.' He dumped his pack on the floor, rooted through it. 'Look.'

Christa looked. 'What is it?'

'Old diary.'

'Old diary that can't wait.' She looked at him. 'Who wrote it – *Hitler*?'

'Stanton Farley Hopwood.'

His mother frowned. 'Hopwood – is he one of the . . . ?'

'It's 1885. Rob says it's Carl's great grandad.'

Christa nodded. 'Sounds about right. So how do *you* come to have it, and why would *I* be interested?'

Harry looked at his mother. 'I think you better sit down, Mum, while I read you something.'

'*Harry,*' sighed Christa. 'I've just got in from work, I'm trying to cook, I haven't *time* to sit down and be read to.'

'It's OK, Mum,' interrupted Bethan. 'I'll see to the rice.'

'Oh, all right.' Christa pulled out a chair, sat down, looked at her son. Harry opened the diary and read:

'October thirteenth: . . . *H threatening to tell her mother unless I name the day. Silly little fool surely can't imagine Father's plans for me include marriage to one of his hands.*'

He looked up. Christa's lower lip was caught between her teeth. She didn't say anything.

'There's other stuff,' he said, 'but I'll cut to October nineteenth. It says:

'*Desperation. We're to meet at the mill at nine p.m. tomorrow when, God willing, all will be resolved.*'

'At the mill,' murmured Christa, staring at her hands on the table.' She looked up. 'Is there more?'

Harry nodded. 'Yes, Mum. The next day he writes:

'*It is done. I do . . . bla, bla, bla . . . but she drove me to it. Soon the rising waters will conceal my crime . . .*'

He broke off, looked at his mother. 'It goes on, but . . .'

Christa nodded. Her cheeks had paled, her hands were fists on the table. 'That's enough, Harry. Thank you.' Her voice was husky, almost a whisper. 'You didn't tell me how you come to have the diary.'

'Carl brought it to school, Mum. He left it in the boys' lavatories by accident and Rob found it. He thought you should see it.'

His mother nodded. 'Yes, well.' She stood up, gazed through the twilight window. 'Obvious who H was, I think.' She looked at her watch. 'I'd better phone Fox at the *Echo*. Hope he's not gone home.'

SEVENTY-FOUR

Monday, seven p.m. As the Rover crunched off down the drive, Carl trailed along the corridor to the conservatory, where his mother was trimming palms.

'Mum?'

'Yes, Carl?'

'I've done something. I didn't mean to, it was an accident, but I don't know what to do.'

Felicity sighed, dropped the secateurs into her pinny pocket. 'Why don't we sit down, Carl, and you can tell me all about it?' She led him to where a glass-topped table stood between a pair of wicker armchairs, letting a handful of shrivelled leaves fall into a bin in passing.

'Now,' she said when they were seated, 'tell me what you've done that's so terrible.'

Carl shook his head. 'It's not funny, Mum. I don't even want to tell you, but I have to 'cause I daren't tell Dad. He'd *kill* me.'

His mother arched her brow. 'Not *kill*, darling, surely?'

'Yes, *kill*. I've dropped the family in it, and you *know* what he's like about the family.'

His mother sighed. 'Well, come along – *tell* me about it. I'm sure it's not *nearly* as awful as you imagine.' She looked at him. 'Things always get sorted out you know, in the end.'

Carl snorted. 'Not *this*, Mum.'

He told how he'd trespassed in the office. Rooted through the archive. Found his great grandfather's diary. Forced its lock. Read the faded entries. 'That bit about hands, Mum – you said it sounded Victorian – it's in the diary. And there's more.'

His mother listened silently as he outlined the later, terrible entries. When he told her he'd lost the diary at school her cheeks paled. And when he'd finished they sat tense and unhappy under the palms, waiting for Dad to come home.

SEVENTY-FIVE

'Newsroom.'

'May I speak to Mr Fox? My name's Midgley.'

'Hang on. *Stan – lady for you. Name of Midgley.*'

'Hi, Ms Midgley. How can I help you?'

'You talked about the need for evidence, Mr Fox. Hard evidence. I have it for you.'

'You *have*? Uh . . . in what form, Ms Midgley?'

'It's a diary. I know now that the bones at the old mill belong to Hettie Daynes, and that she was murdered. I also know who killed her, and why.'

'Wow! Seems you've beaten me and Steve to it,

231

Ms Midgley. Can I come round straight away, take a look at the diary?'

'Of course, that's why I rang. I'll put the kettle on.'

Bethan's eyes shone. 'I'll do the kettle, Mum.'

'And I'll plate up some choccy bikkies,' volunteered Harry. He grinned. 'I can't wait to see Councillor Hopwood's face when he looks at this week's *Echo*.'

Their mother shook her head. 'This isn't a celebration, you know. Reginald Hopwood's grandfather ruined an ignorant young girl, then destroyed her like an unwanted dog. We're looking at real-life tragedy, not a TV soap.'

Fox must have broken several records and a couple of laws, driving up from Rawton. He accepted tea from Bethan, a biscuit from Harry and the diary from Christa.

'Stanton Farley Hopwood,' he mused. 'The councillor's grandfather. Sat in the council chamber for years – a churchgoer, a pillar of the community, a fornicator and a murderer. Nobody knew. Unless . . .'

Christa looked at him. 'Unless . . .?'

'Well.' Fox shrugged. 'I suspect the family

knew, else why has my pal Reginald been so keen to keep everybody away from the reservoir since the water level dropped?'

'Yes,' said Harry, 'and why did Carl say *get on the wrong side of a Hopwood and you'll find yourself in deep water?* Or is that a coincidence, Mr Fox?'

SEVENTY-SIX

Ten at night. The Rover screeched to a stop outside the Hattersleys' home. Rob had just gone up to bed. His parents were watching the news. Reginald Hopwood hurried up the path, banged on the front door.

'Who the heck's *that*, this time of night?' Mr Hattersley hoisted himself out of the easy chair, grumbled his way to the door.

Rob looked out of an upstairs window and recognized the councillor. 'Oh-oh,' he murmured, 'bet I know what *he*'s after.' He headed for the stairs.

Mr Hattersley opened the door. 'Yes, what can . . . ?'

'My name's Councillor Hopwood. Is your son in?'

'Y . . . yes, he's gone to bed. Is something wrong?'

'Yes, something's wrong.' Hopwood's eyes stared, his shiny face was purple. 'Your son stole something belonging to my son. This morning. At school. I want it back.'

Rob's father shook his head. 'I don't think my lad . . .'

'It's OK, Dad.' Rob joined his father in the doorway, looked Hopwood in the eye. 'Yes, Councillor, I took your granddad's diary. *Read* bits of it as well – the interesting bits.' He smiled. 'I don't wonder you want it back.'

'You'll give it back *this instant*, or I'll call the police.'

Rob shook his head. 'Not a good career move, Councillor. Anyway, it's not here. I passed it to the family of the murdered girl.'

'*Rob?*' His father plucked at Rob's sleeve. 'What's all this about? *What* murdered girl – it's like something on the telly.'

'Family – *what* family?' roared Hopwood, trying to barge his way past the pair, who stood firm. 'There *is* no family. She was nothing but a—' He broke off.

Rob finished the sentence for him. 'Nothing but a hand.'

Mrs Hattersley appeared between husband and son. 'What's all this *shouting*?' she cried. 'You'll wake the whole neighbourhood.'

'It's all right, Mum,' soothed Rob. 'The councillor's just leaving.' He looked at the apoplectic Hopwood. 'The family's seen the diary, *and* the skeleton at the mill. She was nothing but a mill girl, but they—'

'*Skeleton?*' croaked Hopwood. He swayed, grabbed the lintel to keep from falling. 'There's a—' He pointed a shaking finger at Rob. 'You . . . I'll settle you later, boy, you can depend on it. Not now though . . . matters to attend to. Priorities.' He turned, lurched towards the Rover.

Mrs Hattersley called after him, 'I really don't think you should drive, Mr Hopwood.'

The councillor swung round, pointed at her. 'Shut your stupid mouth, woman.'

They stood on the step and watched him roar away.

SEVENTY-SEVEN

'Is it Mrs Midgley?'

'Yes, who's this?'

'Rob – Harry's mate. Listen. Councillor Hopwood's been here, after the diary. I told him the murdered girl's family has it. He went ape-shape and drove off. I didn't give him your name, but Carl might've mentioned Harry. I thought I'd better warn you.'

'Did you mention the *bones* to him, Rob?'

'Yes I did. I said the family's seen the diary *and* the skeleton. He nearly passed out.'

'Think carefully, Rob – did he *say* anything?'

'Not really. He mumbled something about stuff to do – priorities.'

'I'm going to hang up, Rob – I think he might have gone to the reservoir.'

'The res – *why*, Mrs Midgley?'

'To dispose of the evidence of course. He failed to recover the diary, but without the bones the diary's just words. I'm off now – bye.'

SEVENTY-EIGHT

Christa rapped on her son's door. 'Harry – are you in bed yet?' It was ten o'clock.

'Just going, Mum.'

'Go downstairs, grab a bin bag, we're off out.'

'*What?*'

'Just *do* it, Harry.' She hurried to Bethan's room. 'Bethan, wake up sweetheart, *listen.*'

'Whu . . . ?'

'Harry and I are off to the reservoir. We won't be long. I want you to drop the latch behind us. Don't leave the house, don't let anybody in. All right?'

'Suppose so, but why're you . . . ?'

239

'I'll explain later, love.'

Harry was in the kitchen, ramming a black bag in his pocket. 'What *is* it, Mum – you finally flipped or what?'

Christa grabbed a jacket, shrugged into it. 'Hopwood,' she gasped, 'after the bones. My poor aunt suffered enough, at the time and since. He'll not rob her of a decent burial.' She strode to the foot of the stairs. 'You coming down, sweetheart?'

Bethan appeared at the top, looking bleary. Christa smiled. 'Good girl. Lock up straight away, won't you?'

When Bethan reached the kitchen, they'd gone. She dropped the latch and stood barefoot on the tiles, knuckling her eyes.

Then she padded across to the phone.

SEVENTY-NINE

He stood, shoes full of ooze, in the yard of Hopwood Mill. The moon was a smudge in a veil of cloud. The mist made everything look the same. He'd pulled a thick, rotten branch out of the mud. With this he slashed at the mist, turning and turning, half-blind with tears. 'My name's Councillor Hopwood,' he choked. 'Matters to attend to, get away, get away.'

He'd searched everywhere. Wall bottoms, heaps of broken stones. No bones. When one thing goes wrong everything does – he'd left a powerful torch in the Rover. Now he was hearing voices.

Voices. He crouched in shadow by a bit of wall, breathing hard, staring at haze. It was after ten on a chill November night, who'd come here? Busybodies, that's who. Folk with nothing better to do, like that scruff with the magazines. He grasped the branch and held his breath.

'It's this way, Mum – come on.'

'*Wait*, Harry, he'll be here somewhere, don't get too far ahead.'

'There's nobody, Mum, listen – dead quiet.'

Harry reached the first wall and cried out. A figure loomed, shadow out of shadow. He flung up his arms to ward off a blow but the shape barged past him, Neanderthal, brandishing a club, shambling towards his mother.

'Mum, watch out!' He ran after the thing but it reached Christa, flung a thick arm round her neck, raised its club.

'Stop!' Hopwood bared his teeth at the boy. Harry stopped dead, gazing into the eyes of a madman.

'L-let her go,' he cried. 'The police are on their way.'

The councillor laughed. 'No they're not.' He flexed his arm, constricting the woman's throat.

She gagged. 'Show me where the bones are, or I'll throttle this slag like the nobody she is.'

'Yes, OK.' Harry nodded wildly. 'They're here, see – just here, under this pile of stones.'

'Shift the stones,' snapped Hopwood. 'Hurry up.' He squeezed a dry cough out of Christa. Harry bent, picking up stones, throwing them aside. He cared nothing for the bones, only his mother. The councillor watched closely, his glistening face next to Christa's frightened one. The cloud veil slipped from the face of the moon and there, suddenly, was the pale glint of bone. With a snarl, Hopwood threw his hostage to the ground and stood over her, the branch raised high against the moon.

'No – *don't*!' croaked Harry. 'You've got the bones – you promised.'

'Hah!' Hopwood barked a laugh. 'I promised nothing. It's ladies first, then brats.'

He raised the club as high as he possibly could. Mother and son closed their eyes.

EIGHTY

'Eeeeeaagh!' His mother's scream shocked Harry's eyes open. Blood and splintered bone she'd be. A pinkish pulp, pulsating.

He blinked and gasped, unbelieving. She was whole, propped on an elbow. She hadn't screamed – her assailant had.

The shade of Hettie Daynes stood over its bones, on nothing. It made no sound and its gaunt features were impassive, yet its fury seemed to crackle on the air, directed at the hulk that grovelled whining in the mud as though impaled on that thin, accusing finger.

'I'm sorry,' babbled the councillor. 'So sorry

244

for ... everything. Yes that's it, for *everything*. Stop pointing, don't look at me like that, *do you know who I am?*'

It seared him, that fury. Dammed for a hundred years in dim green silence, it poured like lava through his shuddering carcass. He wept and wailed and beat his head on the mud while the shade looked on, unmoved.

'Harry?' whispered his mother. She was kneeling now, starting to get up. 'Do you *see* her?'

He nodded. 'Yes, Mum.' He couldn't look away. 'She's guarding her bones,' he murmured, 'and her baby's. She always has.'

The spectre did not react to their voices, they might not have been there at all. But Reginald Hopwood heard, and lifted a mud-streaked face. 'Get her off me,' he croaked. 'Please. Make her go.'

'She isn't touching you,' said Harry. 'She can't, and she wouldn't if she could. Get up, she won't even move.'

As the councillor shifted to obey, Harry noticed that the four of them were no longer alone. The mist had thinned to the point where the shore was visible, and there in a line stood

Stan Fox, Steve Wood, and his sister in her dressing gown. From the reservoir's west end, wearing fluorescent jackets, came the policemen Bethan had called. A torch beam swung, skimmed the mud, came to rest on the unhappy councillor.

Hettie Daynes faded and was gone, this time for ever.

EIGHTY-ONE

They buried her bones in a corner of the churchyard, under the bare branches of a shapely beech. The tree had sprung from a nut hidden there by a squirrel in the month of Hettie's death, though nobody knew that.

Everybody was there. Well – *nearly* everybody. Reginald Hopwood had resigned from the council and had left the village at once. In fairness, it must be pointed out that he was blameless in the matter of Hettie's death: if we were to be held responsible for the deeds of our ancestors, we would *all* have bloody hands. He was a difficult man to live with though, and

247

Felicity had chosen not to go on trying. She and Carl were still at Hopwood House, but they were busy packing and sent flowers to represent them. Oh – and *The Big Issue* man wasn't there. We don't shun unwed mums any more, but we have other outcasts and the shame is ours, not theirs.

Steve Wood and Stan Fox published a brilliant piece in the *Echo* about Hettie, her ghost and her murderer, with snapshots by Bethan Midgley. This had the short-term effect of making Bethan and her three friends famous in the village, and the long-term effect of killing off once and for all the expression *daft as Hettie Daynes.*

Time has passed. The diggers and dumpers have finished their work and departed. Swollen by winter rain, streams and rills have refilled Wilton Water to its fringe of reeds. The ruined mill lies underneath its dark surface, but now no ruined spectre stands upon it.

A stone marks the place where Hettie sleeps with her unborn child, cradled in the roots of the beech. On the stone these words appear:

𝕳𝖊𝖙𝖙𝖎𝖊 𝕯𝖆𝖞𝖓𝖊𝖘
1868 – 1885
𝕬 𝕳𝖆𝖓𝖉 𝖆𝖓𝖉 𝖆 𝕳𝖊𝖆𝖗𝖙

ABOUT THE AUTHOR

Robert Swindells left school at fifteen and worked as a copyholder on a local newspaper. At seventeen he joined the RAF for three years, two of which he served in Germany. He then worked as a clerk, an engineer and a printer before training and working as a teacher. He is now a full-time writer and lives on the Yorkshire moors.

He has written many books for young readers, including many for Random House Children's Books. *Room 13* won the 1990 Children's Book Award and *Timesnatch* won the Junior Category of the 1995 Earthworm Award. *Abomination* was shortlisted for the Whitbread Award and won the Sheffield Children's Book Award. His books for older readers include *Stone Cold*, which won the 1994 Carnegie Medal, as well as the award-winning *Brother in the Land*. As well as writing, Robert Swindells enjoys keeping fit, travelling and reading.